THE BOYS NEXT DOOR

When Ross Anderson and his lively nephews move in next door to Alison Grainger, it ends her well-ordered life — a life that doesn't include children. The noise is bad enough, but Alison becomes critical of Ross's method of childcare even as she becomes attracted to him. She becomes involved in their welfare despite herself. But when it emerges that the boys' grandmother has persuaded Alison to record Ross's progress with the children, the rift between them gets even bigger.

Books by Janet Chamberlain
in the Linford Romance Library:

DANCE WITH ME

JANET CHAMBERLAIN

THE BOYS NEXT DOOR

Complete and Unabridged

LINFORD
Leicester

First published in Great Britain in 2007

First Linford Edition
published 2008

British Library CIP Data

Chamberlain, Janet
    The boys next door.—Large print ed.—
    Linford romance library
    1. Neighbors—Fiction 2. Love stories
    3. Large type books
    I. Title
    823.9′2 [F]

    ISBN 978–1–84782–180–5

Published by
F. A. Thorpe (Publishing)
Anstey, Leicestershire

Set by Words & Graphics Ltd.
Anstey, Leicestershire
Printed and bound in Great Britain by
T. J. International Ltd., Padstow, Cornwall

This book is printed on acid-free paper

New Neighbours

Thwack! The football rocked the garden fence yet again, and Alison Grainger groaned and banged her coffee mug down on her desk. This wasn't her day. Her cat had gone missing, her computer was on the blink, and now her new neighbour's three young boys were giving a whole new meaning to the word rumbustious.

From the moment they'd moved in a couple of days ago, those kids had alternated between slamming their football against the fence, yelling themselves hoarse, and trampling Alison's cherished flower beds every time they climbed over the fence to get the ball back. How much more could she take?

With a sigh, she reached for the framed picture that she kept on her desk. 'No wonder you've run away,' she told the wobbly drawing of a smiling marmalade cat. 'Those kids are enough to scare anyone.'

But despite her annoyance, she couldn't resist a tiny half smile as she looked at the picture. Her son, Ben, had been only two years old when he'd drawn it. A stranger might need an act of faith to tell what it was, but she remembered Ben's precious voice explaining to her that the mass of orange scribble was in fact Pusskins, their family cat.

'Come home soon, Puss,' she whispered, tracing her finger over the wiggly outline. 'I couldn't bear to lose you, too.'

A raucous cheer from outside forced her attention back to her neighbours.

With great care, Alison returned the picture to her desk and then stood up and headed for the front door.

When they'd first moved in, she'd decided to give the boys a couple of days' grace to run riot while they settled into their new surroundings, but that time had just run out. With a new client due in half an hour, she couldn't risk any more yells and thwacks. But she hadn't even reached her front door when an ominous crash sent her dashing back to her office.

Just as she'd feared — a scuffed leather football sat beneath the window, surrounded by shards of broken glass.

But it wasn't the broken pane that caused her heart to chill. On the floor, in a puddle of coffee, was her treasured drawing — its glass shattered into a thousand pieces; hot, brown liquid seeping through the splintered glass.

'No!' She choked out the word, her throat aching with dread. This picture was special. Irreplaceable. A part of her tiny son.

Hot tears spurting, she fell to her hands and knees. Shook out the glass. Mopped the sopping paper with the sleeve of her blouse.

Too late. Ugly stains marred the drawing's once pristine white background and when she tried to lift the picture free of its backing, the sodden paper disintegrated.

Her heart plummeting to the bottom of her chest, Alison crossed the room and angrily dropped the picture into the bin.

Then, her lips tight, she snatched up her jacket and strode out of the door.

★ ★ ★

Ross Anderson was not having a good day. He turned down the television and stared hard at his three squirming nephews. A fourth little boy was lying, half asleep, on the sofa.

'What do you mean you want to watch TV? Five minutes ago you said this programme was for babies.'

'We've changed our minds.'

Eight-year-old Matt gazed at the carpet and shuffled his feet while his two younger brothers nodded in agreement.

Something was most definitely wrong here. Why were these three macho kids desperate to watch a big blue rabbit sing nursery rhymes?

'Where's your football, Mattie?'

'In the garden.'

Hmmm. And since when had they been so blasé about leaving their favourite football unattended? As a rule, they were too scared of losing the ball to let it out of their sight.

'Go and get it, please. I want to see it.'

'Well, it's not exactly in *our* garden,' Mark offered in a small voice.

'No?'

Luke gave a nervous grin. 'It went over the fence.'

'So, go and ask for it back. I'm sure the nice lady next door won't mind, so long as you're polite. I'll have to go round and introduce myself sometime soon, but I can't leave Jon on his own.'

The boys exchanged uneasy glances.

'We're tired of football,' Mattie said at last. 'We'll play later on when she throws it back. We want to stay inside with you.'

Ross's frown eased. So that was it.

They wanted his company and he'd been too busy to realise. This guardianship lark should come with a user manual, or at the very least a freephone help line.

He hunkered down to bring his face level with theirs. 'Look, boys, I'm sorry. I know you really want me to spend some time with you, but tossing your football over the fence won't alter things.'

He nodded towards the sofa, where three-year-old Jon lay watching TV.

'Your little brother isn't feeling well, and I have to give him my attention for now. Be good kids and go back out into the garden. I'll join you when he falls asleep.'

Poor kids. When he'd broached the idea of them spending a few months holidaying at his cousin's country cottage, he'd really played up the fact that he'd be spending lots of time with them. But Jon coming down with a virus hadn't been part of the plan.

They could have delayed the holiday

until Jon had recovered, of course, but back home the daily visits from the boys' maternal grandmother had fast become a trial. OK, he was new to the parenting game and didn't dispute the fact that he'd made a few mistakes. But to hear that woman talk, anyone would think he was the world's worst guardian. How on earth his brother had coped with her he had no idea.

But this break would give him the chance to pause, rewind and start again.

He needed time to bond with the boys and to gain their trust away from their grandmother's constant criticism and interference.

Yes, he knew that she loved them too. And, yes, he knew he'd taken on a lot. He also knew it was going to be tough for a single guy like him to put his career on hold for several months and then to commit the rest of his life to taking care of these children. But he *was* committed and he didn't regret his decision one bit. And for the moment, his priority was to make sure the boys knew all his promises would be honoured, just as soon as Jon was on the mend.

Mattie screwed up his face. 'It's so hot out there, maybe we should all stay inside and draw pictures. Jon could do that, too, if you found him something to lean on.'

A chorus of agreement.

Jon raised his head and gave a happy grin.

That decided Ross. 'All right. Drawing it is. I'll find some paper and pencils.'

He left the boys sitting together on the sofa watching TV. Those few hours in the fresh air must have worn them out. He'd never known them so quiet.

A loud rap at the door shattered the peaceful atmosphere.

Ross stiffened. Who could it be? Surely the boys' grandmother hadn't decided to visit already? He'd assumed an hour's drive would be more than enough to keep her at bay, but as he strode down the hall to the accompaniment of an urgent series of raps, he was forced to acknowledge that he'd underestimated her. The woman would stop at nothing to have him declared an unfit guardian for the boys. She was probably hoping to catch him off guard when the children were tired and fretful and use the situation to gather more ammunition. Well, this time she'd get her marching orders.

He flung open the door.

Wow! A gorgeous, leggy blonde in a business suit. What did she want? Was she selling something?

'Good afternoon,' he said, his gaze locking with a huge pair of dove-grey eyes. 'How can I help you?'

She glanced past him into the hall. 'We need to talk. Is now a good time?'

Despite her appealing eyes and soft blonde hair, something about her tone sent an ominous shiver down Ross's spine. What was she? A solicitor? A representative from social services?

His own brows drew together in a

frown. He'd done nothing wrong, no matter what that dragon of a grandmother thought. He stepped forward, his large frame barring her way. 'Who's asking?'

She raised her chin and met his gaze. 'Alison Grainger, your next-door neighbour.'

His scowl eased into a smile. She was his neighbour, that was all. There was no court order, no social services. He'd live to fight another day!

'Pleased to meet you, Alison,' he said, his body sagging in relief. 'What have those little horrors done now?'

'Only put a football through my window.'

'Oh . . . I'm sorry. No wonder the little rascals . . . ' His words trickled away. Alison Grainger wouldn't be appeased by a mere apology, that was obvious from her stoney unresponsiveness. He started afresh. 'I'm sure it wasn't deliberate.'

'Maybe not, but that doesn't explain why they have to play outside my window. What's wrong with the other side of your house? There are no neighbours there, just a field of donkeys.'

'And an old conservatory — I'd be worried they'd smash the glass.'

Her lips tightened. 'But it's OK for them to smash mine instead?'

'No, of course it isn't.' He raked his fingers through his hair. 'Please send me the bill for the repairs.'

She closed her eyes for a few seconds. 'There are some things money can't fix.'

'Such as?'

The silence stretched out for so long he wasn't sure she'd reply.

'Noise, for one thing,' Alison said at last. 'And my poor flower beds for another. Every time that ball — '

A bright red gash on her palm caught his attention. 'Hey, you've cut yourself.'

Her hand froze. 'What?'

As he moved forward, the cool, floral fragrance of her perfume swirled around him, invading his senses and

11

sending his pulse rate soaring. He quashed the sensation and caught her wrist.

At the puzzled, uncertain look on her face he took her hand in his and turned it over to inspect the palm. 'It's not the only cut, either. How could you do this and not realise?'

As she snatched her hand away, understanding dawned. The glass from the broken window.

Embarrassed, he flashed an apologetic smile. 'No need to answer that. come inside and I'll find you some antiseptic.'

'I-It's nothing. I'll see to it later. I'm here to talk about your boys' behaviour, starting with the noise.'

A stray strand of hair had fallen across her eyes. Ross itched to touch it. To discover if it felt as silky as it looked. He masked the urge by thrusting his hands deep into his jeans' pockets. What was the matter with him? He'd come across beautiful women before. Why was he reacting like a schoolboy with a crush?

Nothing the exasperated look on her face, he said with a sigh, 'All right, so the kids make a bit of noise. But show me boys who don't. It's what they do, for heaven's sake. It's as natural to them as breathing.'

And didn't he know it! He hadn't been acting Dad for very long and was still feeling his way here. But he wasn't going to admit any doubts to his lovely neighbour.

She tucked the loose blonde strand towards the smooth sweep of hair coiled on the top of her head.

'Then you'll have to persuade them to stop. I'm trying to run a professional accountancy firm here. The last thing I need is a gang of rowdy little boys running riot outside my window.'

The kids were a bit boisterous, he couldn't deny that, but no way were they running riot. This woman was taking her complaint to the extreme.

'Hey, that's a bit unfair! The kids are simply enjoying themselves. That's what holidays are for.'

Alison's small chin tilted at an angle that clearly showed she disagreed.

'So what you're saying is, as long as those little terrors are having a good time, you don't care about anyone else?'

'All I'm saying,' Ross said, trying to be patient, 'is that it's unrealistic to set up a professional office in a residential area and not expect a peep out of the neighbours.'

Her expression shifted from dour to incredulous.

'They were making more than a peep.'

He lifted a hand, then let it fall heavily to his side.

'Look, I'm sorry if the kids are bugging you, but I can hardly banish them to their rooms for the next three months.'

Her eyebrows shot up. 'Three months? You'll be around for the next three months?'

'I'm afraid so.' He offered an appeasing smile. 'I'm looking after the place while my cousin is working abroad. Surely she told you all this?'

'She did tell me that a relation was coming to look after her house,' Alison conceded, a tiny frown creasing her brow. 'But I hadn't realised the arrangement was for three months. And I hadn't expected such a mischievous bunch of boys!'

The description set Ross's mouth twitching. It had been a long time since he'd been classed as a mischievous boy.

'I'm sorry if the arrangement doesn't suit you,' he said, careful not to smile. 'But the chance of an extended holiday in a rural seaside cottage was just too good to pass up.'

She glared at him, her generous mouth pursed in an angry little pout, which for some reason, Ross found very attractive.

'Good for you, maybe. But a mini-disaster for me unless you can find a way to curb your children's behaviour.'

'There isn't much I can do short of binding and gagging them, and I'm

15

certainly not about to do that.'

Two small fists planted themselves on a pair of trim hips.

'Well, we can't continue like this. I'm a single woman, struggling to build a business. I need a reasonable amount of peace and quiet. I don't expect the children to be silent, but they'll have to keep themselves and their ball out of my garden.'

She was single? Ross's imagination did a quick double flip.

'Well?' Again, that enticing little pout.

Ross chewed his lip. What could he say? Nothing, he guessed, that would make Ms Alison Grainger's generous mouth curve upwards in a smile. But he was prepared to meet her halfway.

'OK. I don't know what my cousin will say about it but I'll put up a higher fence if you'll give me a couple of days. That should keep the football out of your way.'

Her frown eased a little. 'And the noise?'

Gorgeous or not, she wasn't getting

everything her own way. 'I'm sure that will calm down once the boys have settled into their new surroundings.'

Her eyebrows lifted. 'And in the meantime, it doesn't matter if I can't hear myself think — as long as your nephews are having fun?'

'That's not what I meant,' he said, irritation overriding his attraction to his gorgeous neighbour.

'Didn't you? Well, I'm sorry, but that's what I heard.'

'Then you heard wrong. And another thing . . . ' Ross dashed a look over his shoulder and lowered his voice. 'I'm giving the children a little leeway because — and I would have thought my cousin would have told you this — their parents were killed in a traffic accident only six months ago.'

'Oh . . . '

He watched myriad emotions play across her face. Shock. Dismay. Compassion. Did this brisk, no-nonsense businesswoman have a softer centre than she let on?

'As the boys' uncle and guardian, I take my responsibilities very seriously, believe me.'

She continued her rapid scrutiny, but this time her expression held unmistakable warmth.

'But after what they've been through, you're trying not to be too hard on them?'

'Is that such a bad thing?' His voice was almost a growl.

Her mouth flickered in an admonishing smile. 'Discipline doesn't have to be harsh to be effective. Psychologists say — '

He held up a hand to stop her. 'I've no time for airy-fairy theories.'

To his surprise she didn't back off.

'Then I'm afraid you're in for a struggle. Have you thought of hiring a nanny?'

'A nanny could leave at any time. What the kids need now is permanence. They have that with me and I'll cope.'

A loud wail pierced the air, followed by the sound of angry squabbling.

Alison said nothing but raised an eyebrow at Ross questioningly.

He stared back at her in silence.

The squabbling grew louder.

'Uncle Ross — come quick! Mark and Luke threw our toys all over the room!'

Tense seconds passed. Then, a tiny, unexpected smile lifted the corners of Alison Grainger's mouth.

'Just how long do you plan to ignore what's going on in there?'

'If I wait long enough, they'll settle the battle themselves,' he said, with more certainty than he felt.

Her smiled widened, dimpling her cheeks and revealing a set of perfect white teeth.

'And who'll be the one picking up the toys at the end?'

'Me, I suppose,' he acknowledged with a conciliatory laugh. 'But if the alternative involves yelling at them, then I know which option I prefer.'

'Who said anything about yelling? Surely it's possible to get them to pick up a few toys without needing to raise your voice?'

'And how many children have you brought up, Ms Grainger?' he asked, softening the jibe with a smile of his own.

Her smile disappeared as quickly as it had arrived.

'None, I take it,' he said smugly. 'So maybe you should let me deal with the problem in my own way.' A sudden feeling of devilment prompted him to add, 'Unless, of course, you'd like to step inside and demonstrate your theory?'

Their eyes met and locked.

All her instincts told Alison to turn around and walk away. But if she couldn't get this man to take charge of his nephews, then she was in for a very difficult few months.

She lifted her chin and breezed past him. 'Watch and learn, Mr Anderson. I shall be doing this only the once.'

★   ★   ★

It wasn't difficult to guess which room the children were in. All she had to do was follow the noise down the toy-strewn hall. She paused outside the door feeling panic rise. Maybe this wasn't such a good idea.

'They don't bite, I promise.'

Ross reached across her to push open the door, the warm earthy scent of his aftershave throwing her emotions into a spin.

She blocked the sensation. Those kinds of feelings had died the day her husband walked out of their marriage. Her life was much safer without them.

He gestured for her to go in.

Heart thudding, she stepped forward.

'Right, boys,' he announced. 'This is our new neighbour and she's come to see who's making all the noise.'

'Not me,' said four startled voices, one after the other. Four?

Three pixie-faced imps turned to face her, each with the same thick dark hair and melted-chocolate eyes.

Behind them, a smiling, fair-haired

tot crept out from behind the sofa, a teddy bear clutched in his arms. Alison's heart lurched. The little boy's tousled head and wide-eyed expression reminded her so much of —

She shook her head, quickly suppressing the image.

'Have you brought our football back?' asked one of the imps, earning a swift nudge in the ribs from his bigger brother.

'We didn't mean to break your window,' the second boy put in. 'It just sort of happened.'

Alison took one look at their mortified expressions and an overwhelming feeling of envy welled up inside her. Ross Anderson was so lucky to have four such beautiful children in his life — even if they were a bit unruly.

She cleared her throat. 'Never mind about that. What are we going to do about these toys?'

The boys surveyed the mess.

'It was Mark and Luke who got them out.'

Luke huffed his indignation. 'And you did too, Mattie — and so did Jon.'

Alison picked up one of the empty storage boxes that littered the carpet and handed it to Ross. His eyebrows lifted but he didn't comment. She placed another box next to the boys.

'Let's forget whose fault it is and have a race. When I say 'go', I want you to grab as many toys as you can and stuff them into your box. Your uncle will do the same. He's bigger than you so he can work on his own. The winner is the team who gets the most. Are you ready? One, two, three, go!'

The family lurched into a frenzy of activity, snatching up the toys by the armful and almost falling over each other in their eagerness to drop them in to their boxes.

'Yes!' Jon's eyes danced as the boys' box filled up. 'We're winning, we're winning!'

Alison smiled at his enthusiasm, remembering another small boy with almost the same shade of honey-blond hair and a similar reluctance to pack away his toys. At the mere mention of the word *race*, his tiny pout would flip into a king-size smile and his eyes would light up at the challenge.

She shut her eyes, closing herself off from the memory. Why had she agreed to do this? Why couldn't she simply have walked away?

When she opened them again she switched her gaze to the boys' uncle. He'd entered into the game with almost as much gusto as his nephews, his deep blue T-shirt straining over his wide shoulders as he bent to scoop up the toys.

Did he dig trenches for a living? You didn't get muscles like that from sitting in an office. Of course, he might work in an office by day and spend his evenings working out, but something about the rebellious nature of his ruffled fair hair suggested an office was the last place she'd be likely to find him.

He broke her gaze with a grin. 'Problems?'

Heat shot into her face. 'You're supposed to let them win,' she reminded him in a far sharper voice than necessary.

He straightened up and stood smiling at her.

Her heart tripped. It was a long time since a man had had this kind of effect on her. What was it about him that unsettled her so?

'What are you staring at?' she demanded, hands on hips.

His attractive mouth curved into a slow, unrestrained smile. 'That's the second time you've bitten my head off. I'm just waiting for you to spit it out so I can put it back on my shoulders.'

Willing her cheeks to cool, she turned away, breathing a sigh of relief when he turned his attention back to the toys. This time, his contribution was no more than a token gesture and his nephews emerged clear winners.

'There you are, Mr Anderson,' Alison said, as the boys exchanged triumphant smiles. 'Job completed without anyone

25

needing to raise their voice.'

She felt a tug at her skirt.

'What's our prize?' a small voice demanded. 'Winners always get prizes, don't they, Uncle Ross?'

'They certainly do.' Ross's gaze returned to rest on Alison's face and a wicked sparkle danced in his eyes. 'I wonder what Mary Poppins has in mind?'

She searched her mind for a sparkling reply. What she'd give right now to put up an umbrella and fly away!

Five pairs of eyes regarded her in silence.

What did all kids crave that was easy to give? She had it — adult attention.

'Your uncle will tell you a story.'

'Yes! Come on, Uncle Ross.' The boys tugged at his hand, urging him towards the sofa. 'Can we have one about monsters?'

Ross sent her an admiring look. 'Maybe your theories are worth listening to after all.'

'I prefer to think of them as

strategies.' She looked at him sideways. 'Perhaps you can come up with a similar scheme for keeping their high spirits under control?'

He treated her to another lazy smile. 'Maybe we could think about it together. What are you doing later?'

That was easy. She'd be working — as she had done every evening for the last three years. Work was her life now. All she had left.

'I'm busy. But I'm sure you'll be able to think of something on your own. And in the meantime,' she added, turning to leave, 'you won't mind if I hang on to the ball for a little while longer? I've a new client due and I don't want our meeting ruined by the sound of it crashing against my fence.'

Alison started through the house towards the front door.

'Wait!' Ross called.

She kept walking. Whatever else he had in mind, she didn't want to know.

He caught her up at the end of the hall. 'You said you're expecting a new client. Does that mean you have room on your books for more?'

Her pulse picked up speed. 'You need an accountant?'

'Not exactly.' His mouth tugged into a rueful grin. 'After that performance back there, I'm looking to buy some of your time. I'll pay you your normal professional rate if you'll call round here each day and give me a quick demo of some more of your strategies. What do you say?'

He didn't realise what he'd asked of her.

'I'm sorry, no.' She turned away. Raised her hand to the latch.

'Please?'

His large, warm palm clamped over her fingers. The spacious hallway felt cramped and constricted, and for several interminable seconds nothing registered except the heat from his fingers and the racing of her heart.

She moistened her dry lips.

'Really, I can't.'

'Can't, or won't?' he asked softly, his

brown eyes glinting.

She pushed away a wave of longing. He could charm all he liked, but the answer was still no.

'Won't.' Her voice was firm and final. 'There's no point in sidestepping the issue, Mr Anderson. I find children a trial, and I'll go to any lengths to avoid them.'

The smile slipped from his handsome face.

'In which case, I'm sorry I bothered you. I'd no idea that you didn't like kids.'

She swallowed past a lump in her throat. One tiny crack and her calm equilibrium would be shattered.

'Goodbye, Mr Anderson.'

★　★　★

Alison ran back down the drive. Never had the safe confines of her home appeared so inviting. She caught sight of a smartly-dressed middle-aged woman waiting by her front porch. Her new client — already? She *would* have to come early today of all days, when Alison's office was sprinkled with broken glass.

'Hello! Please come in,' she said, opening her front door and leading the way into her private sitting-room. 'I'd normally have taken you into my office, but my new neighbour's children have broken the window.'

Her visitor perched on the edge of a chair.

'I'm sorry,' she said, with a sad sigh. 'Their behaviour hasn't always been so thoughtless.'

'You know them?' Alison asked after a couple of seconds of puzzled silence.

Another pause while the woman absently tucked a sleek chestnut strand into the chignon twisted at her nape.

'I'm Claire Samuels, the boys' grandmother. I hope you don't mind me dropping in on you out of the blue, but I wanted to ask you a favour.'

So this wasn't Alison's client. A rush of relief sent the breath whooshing from her constricted chest. If she could keep this meeting brief, there would still be time to clear the broken glass and call a glazier. What on earth could this woman want with her anyway?

Alison reached into her pocket and drew out a card. 'I'm sorry, Mrs Samuels — '

'Please . . . call me Claire.'

Alison nodded, and held out the card. 'I can't chat now, I'm expecting a client. My name and phone number are on here, if you'd like to call me later.'

As Claire took Alison's card and glanced over the details, her tense expression melted into relief.

'A professional qualification. That's good — it shows a certain integrity.'

Alison glanced at her watch. She didn't want to be rude but she really didn't have time to sit and make small talk with this woman.

'I'm sorry to rush you but I really — '

'Please . . . two minutes is all I'm asking.'

Something about the woman's earnest expression prompted Alison to agree.

'Two minutes,' she repeated, sinking into the opposite chair, 'but that really is all I can spare.'

Her visitor flashed her a grateful smile. 'In a nutshell, I'm planning to apply for a residency order for my grandsons. I don't feel their uncle is looking after them properly and if I can prove it, there's a very good chance I'll be able to have them live with me.'

A brief wave of regret crossed Alison's mind. For an instant she pictured the fondness in Ross's expression as he'd regarded the boys. Whatever his shortcomings, there was no doubt about his affection for them.

'I don't quite follow. What does this have to do with me?'

'While the boys were living near me,' Claire continued, her voice laden with concern, 'it was easy to keep a close watch on the situation. But now they're here on an extended holiday that's no longer possible. I was wondering if you could . . . I'm sorry, I know I probably seem a bit unbalanced, turning up on a stranger's doorstep like this and asking you to spy on your next-door neighbour. But when I found out that Ross was bringing the boys here while his cousin was away, I . . . Well, I did a bit of reconnaissance and I'm afraid I've been doing some spying of my own! I couldn't help noticing, every time I've passed by here, that the boys must be proving a trial to you and I hoped that perhaps . . . '

'No.' Alison could see at once what was coming. 'If you're asking me to keep a check on things, I'm afraid I can't. Mr Anderson and I don't see eye to eye. I'd prefer to keep my distance.'

A wry smile touched the woman's lips. 'I can understand that. He and I don't hit it off either. But maybe you could talk to the boys now and again, just a few words over the fence and find out how things are going?'

Something niggled at Alison.

'If their uncle's as hopeless as you say, why are they living with him and not you?'

The woman's expression turned troubled.

'My daughter and son-in-law named him as the children's guardian in their wills. At the time the documents were drawn up, I was a widow and totally dependent on my career. It involved vast amounts of travel and was completely incompatible with family life.' Her voice faltered. 'My daughter and son-in-law clearly thought Ross was a better choice.'

Alison's tone softened. 'They probably felt they couldn't ask you to sacrifice your job.'

'They couldn't have been more wrong.' Tears sparkled on the woman's lashes. 'I'd have given it up in an instant. I think the world of those boys.'

Alison's heart went out to her. 'I can see that finding out that your grandsons were to live with their uncle must have come as a terrible shock.'

The woman brushed the tears away

and attempted to smile.

'When Ross took over their care, I told myself it was for the best. That an energetic young man in his thirties was much better suited to the job than a fifty-something grandmother. But since then . . . ' She broke off, choking on the words. 'I've realised that he hasn't a clue how to look after them and I'm determined to have them with me.'

Alison shook her head. She reached over and squeezed the woman's hand. 'Don't get me wrong — but four growing boys would be a huge financial drain. How would you manage if you gave up work?'

This time the smile was broader.

'I gave up my job a few months ago, when I married the most amazing man.'

'And he's keen to have the boys?' asked Alison.

A tender light filled her visitor's eyes.

'Absolutely. He's financially secure, loves children, and I know that together we can give those poor boys all the care and attention they need. That has to be better than their uncle's misguided attempts.'

There was no disputing that. Although Alison admired Ross for stepping into the surrogate parent role, he seemed so out of his depth. Those kids would be much better off with this strong woman at the centre of their lives.

'The boys are lucky to have such a caring grandmother.'

'So you'll help me?'

What could she say? Alison had meant it when she'd told their uncle she found children a trial. Being around them brought such a feeling of loss, she'd sooner avoid them altogether. However, that information was something she had no intention of sharing with a total stranger.

While Alison raked her mind for an acceptable reason to refuse, Claire Samuels opened her bag and took out a small, hard-backed notebook, followed by a card bearing her name and address.

'I'm not asking you to go round there, or even to talk to them if you'd rather not. But if you could just keep your eyes open and jot down anything at all that worries you? It could make such a difference to the boys' future.'

Alison swallowed hard. When she'd been growing up, her parents had taken in foster children; many from large families and disorganized homes. She'd seen more than enough victims of misguided parenting to know Claire Samuels' worries were very real. It had taken months to settle their frustrated and confused little guests into the family routine. Nightmares had been frequent, tears and tantrums even more so. Although she'd only just met her young neighbours she would hate them to end up feeling so insecure.

'What sort of things did you want to keep an eye on, exactly?'

Her visitor gave a deep, shaky sigh. 'Not feeding them properly, not controlling their behaviour, no set bed times, let alone baths before them.'

Alison glanced again at the woman. Despite their lack of discipline, the children seemed well-fed and happy. Was Ross a neglectful guardian? Or was the boys' grandmother exaggerating? Not knowing much about either, it was very difficult to say.

Maybe she ought to keep an eye on the family, just in case?

The doorbell chimed.

'That'll be my client,' she said, glad of an excuse to end the conversation. 'Perhaps we can discuss this some other — '

'Please?' the woman persisted, holding out the book. 'You can't imagine what it's like to lose your child, then find yourself denied . . . '

The look of anguish in her eyes connected with Alison so fully, she couldn't bring herself to refuse the request outright.

'Leave it with me,' she heard herself saying. 'I'll think about it.'

Screams In The Dark!

The rest of that afternoon and evening, Alison fell into her usual routine. Her new client seemed impressed; a glazier boarded the broken window; and the noise level from the little terrors next door gradually dwindled away to a blissful silence.

'I still have their football,' she remembered. They would get it back once she'd caught up with her work, but they needed to learn that bad behaviour had consequences.

Stifling a yawn, she checked her office clock. Nearly midnight. But even the bone-crushing weariness of a sixteen-hour day was better than the alternative — too much time to dwell on the past.

Her eyes misted as she remembered how things used to be, before work had become the only thing in her life that mattered to her.

She dashed away the tears. What was wrong with her? She hardly ever cried these days. Were these disturbing emotions a repercussion of her meeting with Ross Anderson and his four little nephews?

What if they were? The situation was only temporary. The family next door would have moved on in a few month's time, then Alison could focus on safe, predictable things — such as her home, her career, and her cat.

Oh goodness, her cat! Forget the goings-on next door. What about poor Pusskins?

Forcing her weariness aside, she rushed to the kitchen and opened a tin of food.

'Come on, boy,' she called, pulling open the back door. 'Dinny-dins! It's your favourite!'

Silence.

She banged the saucer with the spoon. If he were around he'd surely answer to the sound that never failed to bring him running.

Still no cat.

She slumped on to the step. 'Oh, please come home,' she whispered into the darkness. 'You're my last link with Ben.'

She closed her eyes, tears seeping from beneath her lids. Greg had brought Pusskins home on their first wedding anniversary, tucked into the folds of his jacket. Then, as he'd prised the tiny kitten from the warmth of his chest, it had jumped straight into Alison's arms.

It had been love at first sight for her, and when Ben was old enough to take notice, he'd loved Pusskins as much as she had. Between them they'd spoilt the cat rotten, turning him into a total homebody.

She snapped her eyes open. So what had happened to him? A traffic accident? A tussle with a fox? She refused to even consider those possibilities.

The simplest explanations were the

most likely. A lonely old lady had enticed him away. Or he was trapped in a deserted building.

She jumped to her feet. That was it! Instead of sitting here brooding, she ought to be calling for Pusskins from the other end of the garden — by her neighbours' old wooden shed.

★ ★ ★

'No way!' Ross declared, setting three mugs of hot milk on the kitchen table. 'You and your brothers are going to bed.'

'But, Uncle Ross,' Mattie said, his small chin quivering with indignation, 'you promised that we'd all play in the garden just as soon as Jon was asleep.'

Ross glanced at his nephew and gave a quick grin. 'Nice try. But I meant during the afternoon — not in the middle of the night.'

'But we were asleep too, in the afternoon,' he protested. 'Come on, Uncle Ross, you know that's not fair.'

Ross swallowed a brisk retort. The kids were right — he had promised. And if he went back on his word now, he would lose their trust.

'Please, Uncle Ross. We don't have school tomorrow.'

Sighing, Ross opened the door. What harm would it do? The parenting police wouldn't storm the garden just because he'd let the boys play outside in the dark.

'All right, you've got two minutes to hide and then I'm coming after you. One turn each with the flashlight and then bed.'

Mark whistled in astonishment. 'You mean it?'

'Of course I do. What are you waiting for? Go! Go! Go!'

With an excited whoop, Mark raced through the open door, Matt and Luke hot on his heels.

Ross paused to find a torch, then flicked off the kitchen light, the sudden darkness triggering a fresh bout of yells and shrieks.

Alison froze in her tracks. Had Ross finally lost his cool and banished the boys to the garden; turned from push-over to tyrant in a few short hours? Stress could do the strangest things —

Another scream split the air.

She dropped her saucer and spoon and ran towards the fence. What was he playing at? Didn't he realise the kids were scared?

It took only seconds to duck through the gap in the fence, but she hadn't reckoned on finding a tangle of leafy shrubs in her path. Head down and eyes closed, she forced her way through the foliage, arms raised to protect her face from the branches.

She didn't notice the small boy barrelling towards her.

'Uh!' The impact almost knocked them both off their feet. Alison's hand flew out to steady the startled child.

The moment her fingers closed over

the slender shoulders he threw back his head and let out a fifty-decibel scream.

Alison opened her mouth to reassure him, but the collision had knocked the breath from her body, and all she could manage was a feeble gasp.

Arms and legs flailed. Tiny fists lashed out.

'Heeeelp!'

Still struggling to speak, Alison tightened her grip. If she let go now, he'd lunge into the hedge and be cut to ribbons.

The flailing became more frantic.

'No! No! Get away from me!'

'Uncle Ross! Uncle Ross!' a second voice joined in. 'A big hairy burglar's got Mark and won't let him go!'

Oh great! Now *she* was the one scaring the kids.

'Mark — it's all right,' she called, striving for a calm, confident tone. 'It's Ally from next door. I'm not going to hurt you.'

The little boy paid no attention. With

45

a sudden twist he lunged from her grasp and hit the ground.

'Mark!'

The momentum hurled him into a roll. He came to rest with his body curled in a ball and his hands wrapped around his head.

Swallowing the fear lodged in her throat, Alison dropped down beside him.

'Mark . . . are you all right? Can you speak?'

The poor kid needed a hug. Someone to scoop him up and tell him he'd be all right. But no matter what her precise, clear-thinking mind told her, her arms remained clamped to her sides.

He gave a low moan, rocking from side-to-side.

A cold chill raced down Alison's spine. What had she done?

Light blazed. 'Right, move back, everyone.' This time the voice belonged to Ross. 'Mattie, you stand by me and hold the flashlight . . . up a bit, so it shines on Mark without dazzling him.'

'I'm so sorry,' Alison said, her voice

high and shaky. 'I didn't mean to hurt him. He just came out of nowhere, and when I tried to — '

Ross's hand pressed her shoulder, the warmth of his fingers penetrating the thin material of her blouse.

'Don't worry — this one craves attention. He'll be OK in a couple of minutes.'

She shrugged off his hand.

'How can you be sure?'

'We mothers know these things.'

'This is no time to joke. He's holding his head. What if he's badly hurt?'

'I'm pretty sure he isn't. Kids fall down all the time. They get scratched, bang their heads, but they survive. It all helps to toughen them up.'

Alison's stomach knotted. How could he be so complacent?

She measured her words, not wanting to frighten the little boy. 'He may be concussed. Shouldn't you get him to hospital?'

'We'll see.' Ross knelt next to her and eased his nephew into a sitting position.

'OK, Mark, move your hands from your face and tell me where you hurt.'

Slowly Mark raised his head. 'All over.' The words came out as another low moan.

'Open your eyes and tell me which part hurts the most?'

The boy winced and opened one eye. 'My head . . . I think.'

Ross tipped back the boy's head, examined his face, and then ran his fingers through the tousled mop of hair. 'No lumps or bruises there. Are you sure it's your head that hurts?'

Mark chewed his lip. 'Well, my legs are a bit wobbly . . . ' He wiggled them as if to emphasise the point.

'Anything else?'

He gripped his stomach. 'And my tummy feels really funny.'

'Do you feel sick?'

'Yes . . . No. Sort of.'

Alison held her breath. *Concussion. Definitely concussion.*

Ross leaned back and studied him. 'Would a bowl of ice-cream help?'

A wide smile, followed by a vigorous nod.

'Then you'd better stand up and walk to the kitchen.'

Mark scrambled to his feet, flashed his brothers a smug smile, then scampered off down the path.

The sight brought a sigh of relief rushing past Alison's lips.

'You OK?' Ross placed a hand under her elbow and helped her to her feet. 'Hey, you're shaking.'

Warm hands encircled her arms, sending tiny tingles dancing through her nervous system. What would it feel like to relax against his chest, to let the warmth of his body soothe away her anxieties?

Dismayed by the direction of her thoughts, she took the precaution of moving away from him. Good grief, her heart was pumping a mile a minute. What made her react to him like this? The man was a stranger.

She busied herself brushing imaginary flecks of grass from her skirt.

'I'm a bit shaky, that's all. I'll be fine in a couple of minutes.'

He shot her a teasing glance.

'Would a bowl of ice-cream help?'

Mattie gave a gasp. 'That's not fair! Everyone gets ice-cream but us!'

'We ran to help Mark,' Luke's outraged voice put in. 'We should get a treat, too.'

Ross folded his arms across his chest. 'Let's ask the big hairy burglar, shall we? What do you reckon, Ally? Do they deserve ice-cream?'

She managed a shaky smile. What made her so susceptible to the man? One grin from him and her brain turned to mush.

'I don't see why not.'

'Right. Ice-cream all round it is.'

With a whoop, Mattie pushed the flashlight at his uncle.

'Quick, Luke, before Mark scoffs the lot.'

'Mattie, you dish it up,' Ross called to their retreating backs. 'And if I hear any quarrelling — hide and seek is cancelled.'

As Alison watched the two boys go, a sliver of unease crept up her spine.

'Where's Jon?'

'Asleep on the sofa.'

'You left him in the house by himself?' Her already fragile emotions raised her voice to a squeak. 'But he's hardly more than a baby. What if he'd woken and found you gone?'

'No fear of that — he's truly fast asleep.'

Alison tried to keep the look of dismay off her face. Ross didn't seem the slightest bit worried. Maybe the fault lay with her.

She dismissed the thought as quickly as it had arisen. You could never be too careful where children were concerned. Tragedy could strike anywhere, at any time. Caution and vigilance were essential.

'Have you left a light on for him?'

'Ye-es,' Ross said on a sigh. 'You're the world's worst worrier, do you know that?'

She took a deep, calming breath. The

incident with Mark had shattered her self-control. She needed to be by herself to take stock of her feelings and organise her tumbling thoughts.

'If you're sure Mark is all right . . . ' She heard the wobble in her voice. Cleared her throat. Tried again. 'I'll get off home then.'

'Not so fast.' His voice held the same amused tone he'd used on the boys. 'Haven't you forgotten something?'

'Such as?'

'What were you doing in our garden?'

'I was . . . ' The notion of Ross ordering the boys into the garden as some sort of punishment now seemed too ridiculous for words.

He tilted his head and offered an encouraging smile. 'Digging a moat? Erecting a barbed wire fence?'

She caught her lower lip between her teeth, casting around her mind for a plausible answer. 'Looking for my cat.'

'Of course.' The moonlight revealed little of Ross's expression, but the smile in his voice told Alison that he didn't believe her. 'And you thought it might be here because . . . ?'

'He could have been shut in the shed.'

He gave a low chuckle, triggering a delicious, warm sensation in the pit of her stomach.

She fought the feeling. 'What's so funny?'

'So the minute this idea occurred to you, you felt compelled to scramble through the fence and find out?'

'Yes.'

He crossed to the shed and pulled open the door.

'Well, be my guest. Take a good look around in there.'

She took a deep breath and stalked into the shed, her gaze scanning the moonlit interior for a familiar pair of luminous green eyes. But even before the beam from Ross's flashlight swept into the corners, the silence told her that Pusskins was nowhere around.

'And that was your only reason for being on this side of the fence?'

Disappointment prickled. She'd almost convinced herself that the cat was shut inside the shed. Now Ross forced her to face the possibility that something more serious had happened to him.

She gave a defeated sigh. 'What other reason could there possibly be?'

He clicked off the torch. A shaft of moonlight slanted through the shed window, bathing their surroundings in a silvery glow.

'That you came to complain about the noise?'

'I'm not an ogre — ' she began, whirling to face him.

He must have been standing right behind her. She slammed into his chest, sending the flashlight thumping across the floor.

Strong hands reached out to steady her, the heat of his palms searing the sensitive skin at the tops of her arms.

'No. You're much too good-looking to be an ogre,' he whispered, his breath warm on her cheek. 'But that still doesn't answer my question.'

She shrugged him off.

'I told you the truth — I was looking for my cat.'

The spicy scent of his cologne pervaded the scant inches between them, raising goose bumps over her skin, and Ross lifted a hand to her face, the action sending an unexpected ripple of excitement zinging to every nerve ending. Then, after an interminable, heart pounding moment in which she wondered if he was going to kiss her, he plucked a clump of dry leaves from her hair.

'You surprise me, Ally.' He released the leaves and watched them spiral to the ground. 'I didn't take you for the animal-loving type. I wonder what other surprises you have in store?'

She drew in her breath. 'Nothing as bad as the one I got when I realised you'd sent the boys out to play in the dark.'

He gave a slow, provocative smile. 'Haven't you ever felt the urge to do something unexpected?' His gaze dropped to her lips. 'Even though you knew the idea was crazy?'

A shiver of anticipation skipped down her spine. He *was* about to kiss her, and for some reason she didn't want to analyse, she wasn't going to do a single thing to stop him. What was the matter with her? She'd always prided herself on keeping her emotions in check and now her body undermined her.

'No, I haven't. It's far more important to control your actions . . . to know what's going to happen next.'

The words spilled out in a breathless rush.

Was she talking about the children or herself?

'What I meant to say is . . . those boys need a consistent routine, with ten hours' sleep at the very least.'

Summoning a massive effort of will, she pushed past him and out of the door.

'And they get it.' In a beat he'd caught up with her. 'Maybe not the full ten hours all in one go, but what does it matter if they sleep late in the morning or grab a nap in the afternoon? It's the element of unpredictability that makes life fun.'

Again that devilish smile, sending her pulse rate soaring.

She avoided his gaze, willing her pounding heart to slow. 'For you, maybe. But those kids have only recently lost their parents. To feel secure, they need to wake up to a normal day with a predictable routine and end it with something familiar. Like a story and a relaxing bath.'

He gave an impish grin.

'What's the point in giving them baths when they'll be spending their days on the beach? A dip in the sea is much more fun.'

'Fun! Those boys' lives have been turned upside down and all you can think about is having fun!'

'It's great therapy. In fact *you* should try it. Shake the mothballs off your bikini and set a morning aside to join us.'

A smile touched her face. She could almost picture the scene. A sparkling sea, crying gulls, four laughing boys tumbling in the foaming water — and Ross lying next to her on the sun-warmed sand. For a moment the image was so real she could almost smell the salty tang of the seaweed. She shook her head, annoyed with herself. She could never be part of such a scene.

'It beats sitting in front of a computer,' he added when she made no comment.

Her voice was sharp. 'I happen to like sitting in front of a computer.'

He gave a sorrowful shake of his head. 'You don't mean that.'

'Oh, but I do. Now, if you'll excuse me, I — '

'Have a hot date with a duvet and a cup of cocoa?'

'Something like that.'

'You disappoint me, Ally. What happened to make you so straight-laced?'

The jibe stung.

'Nothing . . . I — '

She turned away. Started walking down the path.

'I just believe in an ordered lifestyle, that's all.'

He caught her arm, whirled her round.

'And you think trapping yourself in a predictable lifestyle is a good way to live?'

Would he never give up?

'I happen to like predictable. Life is short, why take unnecessary risks?'

'So you shut yourself away? Tell me, Ally . . . ' He brushed a strand of wayward hair from her eyes. 'When was the last time you threw caution to the wind and did something purely on impulse?'

She caught her breath and stepped swiftly back.

His voice softened. 'Why work so hard when there's no-one to share the rewards? Wouldn't your time be better spent trying new experiences, making social contacts — '

'Finding a husband, you mean?'

'Why not?' He softened the words with a smile. 'You can't plan to be on your own for ever?'

She felt a tightening in her throat.

'Why not? I have friends. Why should my happiness depend on having a man around?'

He placed his palms on her shoulders and ducked his head to look into her eyes.

'You protest too much. My guess is somebody's hurt you in the past and you're running scared.'

When she opened her mouth to object, he pressed a finger to her lips.

'Put it behind you, Ally. Take a risk on a new relationship, ditch the boring routine and start living for the moment.'

A twist of longing. If only . . .

She raised her shoulders in the barest of shrugs. 'I'm not like that.'

His hands fell away.

'No, you're too busy letting your hang-ups interfere with other people's fun.'

'That's really what you think? That I'm a spoilsport?'

'Just a bit.'

He was so wide of the mark that she felt tempted to open her heart and recount her whole terrible story. But even as the idea entered her mind she knew she couldn't lay bare her most secret emotions.

'Well, you're wrong,' she said, her voice edged with sharpness.

'Prove it.'

'How?'

'By staying and joining our game.' He gave her a lopsided smile. 'I'll even throw in supper.'

★   ★   ★

Ross watched her face with amusement. He needn't have any worries about her accepting. Even in the shadowed moonlight he could tell she didn't think much of the idea. Tension radiated from every line of her body.

Alison glanced down at her skirt. 'I'm

in my work clothes. They weren't designed for . . . '

'Charging through the fence into your neighbour's garden?' He ignored the tiny inner voice telling him enough was enough. 'Don't tell me that wasn't a spur of the moment decision.'

'Of course it was. I . . . ' She hesitated. 'I thought I heard my cat.'

'See, you do have a spontaneous side after all. You just need to practise a little. Now, are you going to seize the moment and risk a game of hide and seek?'

'What do *you* think?'

He couldn't resist temptation. 'I think you need to take a few risks and loosen up.'

It might have been a trick of the moonlight, but for a moment he thought he glimpsed a flash of vulnerability in those large, pale eyes.

'And *I* think *you* need to grow up and take some responsibility.'

Without another word, she turned and headed back towards her own house.

'If you change your mind,' Ross called after her, 'you know where to find us.'

What had made him say that? The woman was anti-kids and anti-fun. He should be looking for ways to keep her on her own side of the fence, not inviting her to join them.

But as he watched her leave all he could think about was how good her warm skin had felt beneath his fingers and how much he'd wanted to kiss her.

* * *

When Alison made her way up to bed that night, she had Claire Samuels' notebook tucked under her arm. The boys' grandmother was right. Ross Anderson had no idea how to look after those kids. He was raising them in a world without routine or order — making fun his only priority.

Alison dropped the book on to the bed, and perched on the stool in front of her dressing-table. Fun! She snatched out the clips anchoring her upswept hair. Was that what had been in his mind when he'd seemed about to kiss her? That he'd take the chance to grab a few moments of impulsive fun?

She picked up her hairbrush and tugged it through her wavy blonde tresses with brisk, vigorous strokes. Thank goodness she had come to her senses. That sort of fun she could do without.

And her neighbours were still out there, Alison realised with a gasp of amazement, as Ross's unmistakable chuckle floated through her open window.

With a disbelieving sigh she got up to close it.

Down in the neighbouring garden, the game of hide and seek had degenerated into a noisy wrestling match. Every so often one of the boys burst from the fray only to be tumbled to the ground by his uncle and brothers in a tangle of arms and legs.

As Alison watched for a moment,

wondering how he planned to calm them down before bed, a tiny, pyjama-clad figure staggered out of the house and across the moonlit grass.

'You left me!' Jon's trembling voice complained. 'I waked up and you'd gone!'

The sight of the bewildered tot tore at Alison's heart. He should be tucked up in bed, not wandering an unfamiliar house, searching for his brothers and uncle.

Shaking her head, she pulled the window tight and closed the curtains.

Then she picked up Claire Samuels' notebook and began to write.

* * *

Popping the tab off a can of cold beer, Ross sank into the comfort of the living-room sofa, every bone in his body aching.

What a day! And to think it had only just ended. His own fault, of course. With the boys' pleas for more games, and then Jon's sudden realisation that he'd been left out of the fun, it had been well past one o'clock before he'd got them to bed.

He shook his head. Poor Jon. He'd been so indignant at being left to sleep instead of being included in the games; but once he'd understood that the next day's trip to the beach depended upon him getting a good night's rest, he'd soon got over his tantrum.

Ross swallowed a sip of beer, letting the weariness overtake him. Two o'clock in the morning and, for the first time in well over twelve hours, he had a moment to call his own. The boys had managed to snatch a couple of hours of sleep during the afternoon, but unfortunately not all at the same time.

But tiredness he could cope with. The ability to survive on limited amounts of sleep was all part and parcel of being a doctor.

No; as much as he hated to admit it, his problem went deeper than exhaustion. How could a man unfazed by working in some of the world's worst war zones find himself so out of his league when it came to looking after a bunch of little kids?

He sighed and rolled his shoulders against the ache.

He'd started out with a simple enough vision. He would raise the boys to be fearless; independent; adventurous. They would never know the meaning of *can't*. And if that called for a bit of healthy neglect along the way, then surely no-one could fault him for that?

Who was he kidding? The boys' grandmother was so convinced his ideas were flawed and dangerous that she was set to call in social services.

He rubbed a hand over his face. He felt like one of those hapless TV quiz contestants — struggling to come up with the right answer, while their opponents waited for them to mess up.

They at least had the option of asking the audience, or phoning a friend. While he, with no family at hand, and a fiancée who'd dumped him the minute he'd agreed to take on his brother's children, had no such safety net.

The kids' grandmother might have little hope of getting the boys, but mud sticks, and her allegations could even damage his career.

He sucked in a breath between his teeth. The forty or so miles between them wouldn't deter her for long. She'd probably rent a caravan on the site by the beach. Then the whole stressful business would start up again.

Maybe he should move further afield. Bring forward his plans to sail around the world. But until the kids learned to respect rules and to pull together as a team, that idea was fraught with hazards.

So, how to achieve his goal of a well-behaved but independently-minded brood? Maybe he should pay more attention to his lovely neighbour's advice. Child-hater or not, she seemed to know a lot about raising kids.

He gave a light laugh. That was a

contradiction if ever he'd heard one. Why would a woman so clearly not the hearth and home type take the time and trouble to become a walking child-care manual? It just didn't make sense.

He sighed and rolled his shoulders again.

Unbidden, tantalising images of wary doe eyes and gently parted lips swam before his eyes. There was definitely more to this opinionated routine junkie than met the eye. It was just as well that his nephews took up so much of his time, or he might be tempted to chase after a few answers.

Locked Out!

When Alison came downstairs the next morning, Pusskins still wasn't home. So what now? Ring a cat-tracing agency? Place an ad in the local paper? Her hand hovered over the telephone receiver.

No. Wait. She needed something more immediate. Such as . . . she gave a slow smile. A batch of computer-printed missing-cat posters.

An hour later, when she left the house to fix a poster to every lamp post, she felt energetic and full of hope.

However, by lunchtime she was hot and frazzled. A whole morning had gone and she hadn't even started her work. She'd better grab a quick lunch, then get cracking.

The sight of a garden centre delivery truck pulling up outside her nextdoor neighbour's house soon put paid to that idea. If Ross put up the new, higher fence as quickly as he'd ordered the panels, she might have only hours to move the plants growing in the border. She couldn't imagine Ross tip-toeing between them as he worked. And if the boys jumped in to help . . . well, the result didn't bear thinking about.

She changed into her oldest clothes, snatched a sandwich for lunch, then spent the rest of the day transferring her plants to the safety of large plastic pots.

She'd been just in time. Minutes after she'd finished, Ross was out there tearing down the old panels. Did that family never rest?

By late evening, her back muscles felt the repercussions of her afternoon's gardening, so after leaving a saucer of food outside the back door in case Puss came back, she headed upstairs for a long, hot soak in the bath.

She'd just lowered herself into the tub when the clink of the saucer tipping against the flags drifted through the open window.

Puss?

She froze. Somewhere in the distance a dog barked, and save for the breeze rustling the bathroom curtains, all was quiet.

Then she heard it again. The unmistakable scrape of china against concrete. Pusskins was home and eating the food that she'd left out for him!

Alison leapt out of the bath, grabbed her big fluffy bathrobe and wrapped it around herself, tying it tight. Then, pausing only to tie a scarf around her damp hair, she raced down to the kitchen and yanked open the door.

Too late! The food was gone and the garden empty.

She stepped outside and padded towards the hedge, the chill night breeze raising goose bumps down her bare neck. 'Come on, Puss!' she called through chattering teeth. 'No need to sulk. I'm here to let you in.'

Something moved along the bottom of the hedge.

Suppressing another shiver, she crept

towards it, then gently parted the branches. The light from the kitchen spilled through the gap, clearly high-lighting . . . a departing hedgehog.

With a dejected shrug, she turned towards the door — only to hear it click shut.

Oh, terrific! Not only was her cat still missing but she was locked out of her house as well.

She took a steadying breath. No point in fretting over something that couldn't be altered. She needed a solution.

Thinking cap on . . . Was there anything out here she could use to break the glass door panel? A gardening tool . . . a brick?

But even as her eyes scanned the garden, she knew the answer. Ever the cautious one, she'd always made a point of clearing away anything that might aid a potential burglar.

So, what about next-door's garden? Ross wouldn't be obsessive about tidying things away. Now the fence was down it would be child's play to slip in and — hold on a minute! Breaking into her house wouldn't be necessary! Several months ago, when she'd been away in London on a course, she'd left a spare key with Ross's cousin and had never asked for it back. She'd thought it would be handy in an emergency to have a key with her neighbour. Well, this was certainly an emergency!

But it would mean approaching Ross again. And did she really have the nerve to turn up on his doorstep wearing a fluffy white bathrobe?

★　★　★

Ross rubbed his eyes. Alison Grainger in a state of undress was the last thing he'd expected to find outside his back door.

He kept his expression blank as he asked her, 'Would you mind explaining your problem again? I didn't quite catch it the first time.'

She curled her bare toes against the

brick step and gave a nervous laugh. 'Sorry. It probably came out a bit garbled.'

She took a deep breath and launched into her explanation again. This time at a slower pace. 'So if you could just get me my key?'

She'd done something different with her hair tonight. Instead of her usual tight, upswept arrangement, golden tendrils spilled from a delicate blue scarf and tumbled across her shoulders in wild disarray.

'Sorry. What did you say?'

'My key? Maybe I should just come in and get it. I know where it's usually kept.'

He hauled his mind back on track. 'Yes, I'm sorry.'

She stepped past him into the kitchen and then stopped, her eyes riveted on a point above the worktop.

'What are you looking at?' he asked as he followed behind her.

She wrinkled her nose. 'That's what I'm wondering.'

He followed her gaze to a large glob of tomato ketchup sliding down the wall, and instantly became aware of the chaos. Dirty dishes filled the sink and discarded take-away packages spilled from every flat surface on to the muddy floor.

Oh no! He'd meant to clear that lot up once the boys were in bed, but tiredness had caught up with him and he'd fallen asleep in the chair.

He took her by the shoulders and steered her through the debris.

'The housework fairy's been on a bit of a go-slow just lately,' he muttered, instantly distracted by the gentle brush of her hair against his knuckles. 'Now, where did you say your key was?'

'This way.' She broke out of his grip and led the way through the sitting room door. 'It's on the mantelpiece under the clock — oh!'

The clock lay on its side on the hearthrug, along with a toppled candlestick and a telltale cushion.

Ross picked up the cushion and

dropped it on to a chair. Those boys were unbelievable sometimes. With no football to kick around, they'd settled for one of his cousin's best cushions — despite the room being out of bounds.

'It looks like someone else got here first.' He set the clock back on the mantelpiece. 'I can't see any key, can you?'

'Lift the rug and check.'

He thrust the candlestick into her hands and did just that.

'Nope. It's definitely not here. One of the kids has probably pocketed it. You wouldn't believe the things they collect.'

She dug her fists into her hips. 'Never mind that. I need my key.'

He turned and leaned one elbow on the mantelpiece.

'I hope you're not suggesting I wake them up, Ms Grainger.' He attempted to look thoroughly shocked. 'Growing children need ten hours of uninterrupted sleep, and so far they've had about two.'

She folded her arms across her chest and scowled at him. 'If you won't wake them up, then perhaps you could see your way to breaking the glass panel in my back door.' She thrust the candlestick back into his hands. 'Here. This should do the trick.'

He fought back a smile. 'After the fuss you kicked up when the kids broke your office window, you're asking me to break another? I never thought I'd live to see the day.'

'Carry on like this and you won't. Will you do it or not?'

'Not.'

She snatched the candlestick back.

'In that case, I'll do it myself.'

'No, you won't.' He placed his hands on her shoulders to prevent her from leaving and felt her body tense.

'Listen,' he said in a gentler tone. 'The sound of breaking glass might prompt a rush of calls to the police station. Do you really want to end up explaining to the boys in blue why you're breaking into your own house?'

She considered his question for a moment.

'Maybe not. But we could pry off the board the glazier nailed to the window frame in my office. It'd be quieter than breaking the door panel.'

'We?'

A helpless lift of her shoulders.

'I don't have the tools. Whereas you have a garage full.'

He tutted. 'But that would mean leaving the boys on their own. I'm surprised you could suggest such a thing.'

She gave a defeated sigh. 'All right, Mr Clever. You've managed to poke holes in everything I've suggested. How about a few ideas from you?'

'Easy.' He whipped the candlestick from her grasp and positioned it beside the clock. 'You spend the night here. And in the morning we find your key.'

She stared down at her bathrobe.

'Something wrong?' He kept a bland demeanour while inwardly enjoying the flush staining her cheeks.

She showed a slight hesitation before answering. 'I don't feel comfortable staying in a house with a strange man when all I've got to wear is a bathrobe.'

He juggled a smile.

'My cousin left a few clothes in the main bedroom. Wear whatever you like.'

'There's no one sleeping there?'

'I'm using the place as a refuge for anything breakable, so it's pretty much out of bounds. Consider it yours until morning.'

Still she hesitated.

He bent to look into her wide grey eyes. 'I hate to point this out, but it's not as though you have much choice.'

She took a slow breath. 'You're right . . . I'm sorry. Thanks for the offer. I'll go straight up now, if you don't mind.'

Why didn't that surprise him?

'Of course not,' he found himself saying to her retreating back. 'Oh, and, Ally . . . '

She turned, her foot already on the stairs.

'Eight out of ten for spontaneity.'

Ten minutes later, dressed in a long cotton nightshirt she'd found in the wardrobe, Alison padded across the floor of her neighbour's spare bedroom. If the door was like her own, she'd find an integral bolt just below the knob. Yes, there it was. Bingo!

She gave a tiny smile of satisfaction as the metal slid into place.

She climbed into the bed, turned on her side and closed her eyes, but she couldn't relax until she heard the click of Ross's bedroom door.

★ ★ ★

Slipping out of one dream and hovering on the brink of the next, Alison stirred in her sleep.

There it was again. A toddler's high-pitched cry.

Jon? She sat bolt upright and strained to listen.

The cries grew more and more frequent until, unable to bear it any longer, she jumped out of bed and opened the door.

A pale light burned on the landing. She stared intently at Ross's door, but despite the shrill frequency of the yells, it remained firmly shut.

She followed the cries to the room next to Ross's. In the soft pink glow of a night-light, she could just make out Jon's restless form surrounded by a discarded quilt and an assortment of soft toys.

Alison tiptoed to his bed. 'Hey, what's the matter?' she whispered.

His eyes fluttered open. 'Uncle . . . Ross?'

The look of expectation in his large round eyes melted the frost in her heart. 'It's not your uncle, sweetie. It's Ally. I came yesterday to help you tidy your toys. Remember? We played a game.'

He nodded and gave a sob.

Without pausing to think about what she was doing, she lowered herself on to the edge of the bed and scooped him into her lap.

'Don't cry,' she soothed, kissing his

damp forehead. 'I know I'm not your uncle, but if you tell me what's wrong, I'll try really hard to fix it.'

He raised his tear-stained face. 'A big, nasty wolf,' he choked. 'Coming to gobble me up.'

She caught herself before saying that such creatures weren't to be found in little boys' bedrooms.

Instead, she rocked his tiny body and stroked his soft hair. 'Why don't I show you how to make it go away?'

He let out a long, shuddering breath. 'Make it go *now*.'

Alison tugged off the scarf from around her hair and pushed a corner into Jon's tight little fist. 'Are you ready?' Then placing her own hand on top of his, she made a series of quick flicking movements with her wrist.

'Shoo, wolf. Shoo! Come on, Jon, you tell him, too!'

'Shoo! Shoo!' His quavering voice grew more confident with each flick of the scarf. 'Go home, wolf! Go! Go away!'

'There you are. All gone,' she said

after one final bout of scarf waving. 'Now, keep this under your pillow, and any time you think the wolf might be around, use it to shoo him away.'

Then, as she lay down behind him and gently eased his head on to the pillow, his tiny thumb slid into his mouth and he snuggled down to sleep.

★   ★   ★

Ross stood on the other side of the adjoining bedroom door, mentally replaying the touching scene. Exhaustion had made him slower than usual to respond to Jon's cries, but his neighbour proved herself to be a great stand-in.

That was if it *was* his neighbour in there. Could that gorgeous voice — so soft and tender it made his chest ache — really belong to Alison Grainger? He gave a wry smile. Maybe the fairies had stolen her away in the night, and left this gentle, maternal creature in her place.

He pushed the door wider and

approached the bed. Yep. It was the same woman. But dressed in that simple cotton shirt, with her soft blonde hair spilling enticingly across the pillow, she looked almost as vulnerable as the child curled beside her.

The gentle rise and fall of her chest signalled that she'd fallen asleep. Ross leaned over and tucked Jon's quilt around her shoulders. She gave a small sigh and snuggled closer to the little boy.

What had happened to the woman who found children a trial? The one who would go to any lengths to avoid them? Maybe the cool businesswoman wasn't quite as cool as she made out, and a warm, child-friendly human being hid under that frosty exterior.

But why should she put up defences at all? With a sigh, Ross took one last look at the adorably mussed hair and gently parted lips, and tiptoed back to his room.

But sleep wouldn't come. Images of Ally chased around his mind, posing questions he'd no means of answering.

Why would such an attractive young woman choose to bury herself in a sleepy seaside village? A middle-aged woman might value the tranquillity. Ally couldn't be more than twenty-eight or nine. Far too young to opt for peace over fun.

And why, when she so clearly wasn't his type, did he find it so difficult to close her out of his thoughts?

After a few hours of tossing and turning he gave up on trying to sleep and got dressed. He'd go downstairs and tackle the unwashed dishes. Nothing like a stack of greasy plates to focus the mind.

He was standing at the sink, waiting for the hot water to clank its way through the ancient pipes, when he became aware of somebody hovering in the open doorway.

'You were late to bed. Go back to sleep,' he called without turning his head.

'It's a bit difficult with all that noise,'

came a cool female voice. 'You surely don't expect the boys to sleep through that.'

Goodbye Ally, hello Ms Grainger.

He turned off the taps and faced her.

She was once more wrapped up in her all-enveloping fluffy bathrobe.

'I don't see why not. If they hear the noise often enough, their brains will learn to ignore it.'

She moved to stand beside him. 'Like yours ignores Jon's nightmares?'

Ross bit his tongue. Now would be a good time to tell her that far from ignoring the kid's screams he'd been out of bed moments after her. But once she realised he'd glimpsed the other Alison Grainger, she would retreat even further behind the barricades, a possibility he was reluctant to risk.

He lounged against the sink, his lazy posture belying the hammering of his pulse.

'What makes you say that?'

'I found the poor boy sobbing in his bed.'

'You went to him?'

He turned back to the dishes and aimed a generous squirt of washing-up liquid into the bowl.

'That was brave, coming from Ms Alison-keep-those-kids-away-from-me Grainger.'

'Never mind that.' Her voice sounded flustered. Uneven. 'Don't you want to know *why* he was so upset?'

'I suppose you're going to tell me anyway.'

'He'd got it into his head that there was a wolf in his room.' She paused to let her words sink in. 'Now where would he get an idea like that?'

Ross started to feel uneasy. 'I can't imagine.'

He snatched a washing-up brush from the window ledge and whipped the water into froth.

'So he hasn't been watching any scary videos?'

He turned to look at her. 'I don't think 'Nightmare On Elm Street' features wolves,' he said with a tinge of sarcasm. 'Now, 'The Howling' on the other hand — ' He broke off at her horrified expression. 'Oh, come on, what do you take me for? A giant rabbit belting out nursery rhymes is about the scariest thing in their collection.'

'So you've no idea where the notion might have come from?'

He rested his palms on the edge of the sink and shot her a sideways look. 'It could have been my bedtime stories, I suppose.'

She gave an I-thought-as-much sigh.

'But you try coming up with something that will satisfy an eight-year-old and not scare a kid as young as Jon.'

'So, what sort of gruesome stories have you been telling them?'

He picked up the frying pan and scrubbed at a coating of congealed fried egg.

'I might have thrown in a few snapping teeth and terrible growls, but who wants a story where nothing happens?'

She made a small, exasperated

sound. 'Three-year-olds are grabbed by simple everyday stories, such as children not wanting to go to bed. The golden rule is — '

He put up a hand, warding off her onslaught. 'OK. I think I get the message.'

She ignored him. ' — to leave them feeling happy and safe. But you've filled Jon's mind with horrible images and left him worried and upset.'

'Phew!' He snatched up a knife and gave the pan a vicious scrape. 'No one will ever die wondering what your opinions are.'

'Please, just listen to me.' Her voice was more than a little unsteady. 'Losing his parents has ripped poor Jon's safe little world inside out. Everything around him feels dangerous, fragile and — '

So tell him something he didn't know. But wrapping the kids in cotton wool wasn't the answer. They wouldn't break into a thousand pieces just because he'd sent a few chills up their spines. Time to bring this conversation to a halt.

He gave her his most charming smile. 'While you're ranting, would you mind passing me some plates? They're on the table behind you.'

Her eyebrows pulled together. 'I don't think you're taking this seriously enough.'

'Of course I am. You're trying to tell me that my scary story might have scarred my young nephew for life. What could be more serious than that? Now, if you don't mind — I need those plates.'

Alison grabbed a stack of plates and swung them towards the sink. 'Here! Now will you please listen to what I'm — oh!' As she let the plates slide into the sink, a fountain of hot soapy water shot up to drench Ross's arms and shoulders. 'I'm so sorry . . . I really didn't mean to do that.'

'Oh, I think you did.' A smile touched his lips. He had her rattled. One push, and he'd break that icy self-control. He scooped up a large handful of suds. 'Start running, Ms Grainger. You have a three-second start.'

'W-what do you mean? I'm only trying to explain — '

He advanced towards her.

'I've had it with your explanations. Now it's your turn to listen to me.'

Disbelief mixed with outrage in her expressive grey eyes.

He edged closer. 'There's nothing wrong with a few scary stories. They help kids face their fears.'

She inched backwards towards the wall. 'Older kids maybe, but very young children lose sight of what's real and what isn't. Jon's far too young for stories about — '

He smiled at the panic in her voice. 'He's old enough to be taught that there are bullies in the world and that banding together can be one of the ways to outsmart them.'

'Maybe — '

'And that if children talk to strangers,

bad things can happen.'

'I suppose . . .'

He backed her against the wall and rested his elbows on either side of her, leaving both soap-laden hands free. 'Then surely it's better if that teaching comes in the guise of Little Red Riding Hood or the Three Little Pigs, rather than something more realistic?'

Her cheeks turned pink. 'Oh . . . fairy tales. I didn't realise.'

He suppressed a smile. 'That's supposed to be an apology, is it?'

An unexpected flash of amusement gleamed in her eyes. 'OK, so I got it wrong.'

'Not good enough, Ms Grainger.' He dabbed suds on the end of her nose.

Her wide mouth split into a grin. 'What exactly do you want me to say?'

'How about . . . that you over-reacted in the extreme, and now you're sorry?'

She made a small, disparaging noise.

He leaned closer, his lips inches from hers. 'I'm sorry. I missed that.'

Challenge lit her eyes. Then, in one

sudden movement, she pushed the remaining suds towards his chin and ducked out of his arms.

'Right. This is war!'

His breath coming rough and quick, he pursued her to the living-room.

'OK. OK. You were right and I was — ' Her words dissolved into a shriek as he caught her around the waist and she fell backwards on to the sofa.

'Carry on, I'm listening . . . ' He pinned her to the cushions, imprisoning her in the circle of his arms.

She moistened her lips with the tip of her tongue. 'I'm sorry — I got it wrong. Will that do?'

'Too late,' he whispered, his mouth brushing hers. 'It's pay-back time.'

Ross Has An Accident

Ross's lips were unexpectedly gentle as they drifted over hers in a bone-meltingly slow kiss that sent tingles of excitement coursing through every nerve-ending in her body.

Her mouth softened as she relaxed beneath him, her resistance melting like the morning frost in the midday sun.

Then, as the kiss deepened, and slowly she raised her arms to thread her fingers through the thick, dark-blond hair at the nape of his neck, he abruptly pulled away.

'Much as I'm enjoying this,' he murmured, resting his forehead against hers, 'we have to call a halt.'

'Oh.' Her voice was a mere croak.

'Don't you hear anything?'

Only the beating of her heart.

'We have visitors,' Ross murmured, removing himself from her embrace.

He hauled himself to his feet and strode to the open door.

The sound of scuttling feet.

'Mark and Luke! I thought as much. What are you two doing?'

'Oh — Uncle Ross!'

Alison got up from the sofa. What was happening to her? At the first brush of his lips all her self-imposed rules had flown out the window. At twenty-eight years old she ought to be capable of a little more restraint.

She took a deep breath. Composed herself. Forced a smile.

Mark looked from Ross to Alison, then back to his uncle again.

'You were kissing. Are you going to get married?'

Ross placed a hand on each boy's shoulder. 'I'm the one asking the questions around here. Why aren't you two in your beds?'

His voice sounded a little strange, as if he'd run out of breath.

'We were hungry.' Luke assumed a woebegone expression. 'So hungry that we couldn't sleep.'

Mark nodded. 'So we came down to get some pizza for ourselves.'

'Well, you're out of luck. I threw all the leftovers in the bin. But now you're here, we have the little matter of the sitting-room to sort out.'

The boys exchanged puzzled looks.

'Who knocked the clock off the mantelpiece?'

Understanding dawned. 'He did!' each said, pointing to the other.

'All right. Try this one. Who took the key that was under the clock? And if you can't remember, poor Ally won't be able to get into her house. That key belonged to her.'

Neither said a word, but a look of unease crossed their faces.

Smiling, Alison crouched to their level. 'I've locked myself out. The key was a spare one that I kept here. It'd be great if you could remember who moved it.'

'It might have been me,' Luke mumbled, after a lengthy pause.

Mark gave a gasp. 'It *was* you. You know it was! You collect old keys. You've got boxes full of them!'

'So where is Ally's key now?' Ross persisted, his eyebrows drawn together in a frown.

Luke traced a toe along the pattern on the carpet. 'It might be in one of the boxes under my bed.'

'So scoot up there and look,' Ross ordered. 'Mark, you go with him and help.'

'Can we have some breakfast first?'

'No breakfast for you until Ally has her key. Now go!'

The boys shot off at breakneck speed, their heels clipping a pile of stuffed animals stacked at the foot of the stairs.

'I'm sorry if the boys embarrassed you,' Ross said, making no move to pick up the scattered toys. 'They've got it into their heads that our family won't be complete until I have a wife, and every woman I meet is viewed as a potential candidate. Next time, I'll make sure we don't have an audience.'

Alison inhaled sharply. 'Next time? What makes you think I want there to be a next time?'

Amusement sparkled in his eyes. 'Your enthusiastic response. Or was I imagining things?'

What could she say? Her face growing warm, she bent to gather an armful of toys. For one rash moment she'd allowed physical attraction to get in the way of common sense. But no way would it happen again.

'Don't you have some washing-up to finish?'

'You're right, I do. Join me for a coffee when you've finished obsessing over those toys.'

'Obsessing! I'm simply trying to prevent an accident.'

She dropped the toys under the hall table, then retraced her steps to pick up one that had escaped the pile. Closer inspection revealed a balding, one-eyed teddy bear, with a faded blue ribbon around its neck.

Slowly Alison turned it over. Ben's teddy bear had been almost identical to this one, but Ben's had had a red ribbon instead of a blue one and its fur hadn't worn away through years of loving — the little scamp had cut it off with his first pair of blunt-ended scissors.

Her throat constricted. Bald or not, the saggy old bear had been his most cherished possession and she hadn't been able to bring herself to part with it. Dusty and neglected, it lay at the back of a cupboard.

Conscious of a sudden silence, she raised her head. Ross stood in the doorway between hall and kitchen, a puzzled expression on his face.

'For someone who doesn't like kids, you seem very concerned about their welfare.'

She cleared her throat. 'Just because I understand their needs, it doesn't automatically follow that I want kids around me.'

'If you've gone to all the trouble of

learning to understand them, why wouldn't you want them around?' He propped his shoulder against the doorpost and crossed his arms. 'Unless, of course, they scare you. Are you a burnt-out teacher, by any chance?'

'No.'

'An only child then?'

'Sort of.' Then, at his bemused expression, she went on, 'My parents couldn't have any more children after me. So they made up for the loss with a succession of foster children. I had a whole batch of surrogate brothers and sisters to keep me company.'

He shot her a knowing smile. 'I bet you often found yourself hauling them out of scrapes? Maybe found them a bit of an irritation at times?'

Had she? Her mother had sometimes given her extra pocket money to amuse them, and the extra responsibility had made her feel really grown up. But she'd enjoyed the challenge and had learned to handle kids in the process. Had looked forward to doing it all again with a family of her own.

'Irritation? I — '

He cut her off with a laugh. 'It's all right to admit it.' He retraced his steps and perched his large frame on the edge of the hall table. 'My brother was two years younger than me and was a right little tear-away. The responsibility of keeping a brotherly eye on him got a bit much at times. But once you're older, everything changes.'

'Younger brothers eventually stop jumping on the bed and roller-blading in the kitchen?' she asked, keeping the mood deliberately light.

A deep low chuckle. 'There is that. What I meant is — your perspective changes and you begin to realise that kids can be a pleasure as well as an irritation. If you took the time to get to know my nephews you'd soon see what I mean. Why not give it a try?'

For a moment, her imagination took flight and she pictured Ross and his boys on cycle rides, fishing trips, playing football in the park — and herself in the thick of it, relishing every moment. Then the sensible, clear-thinking part of her brain kicked in and her excitement drained away. With this man's carefree approach to life, how long before something terrible happened and her world disintegrated again?

She turned away.

'Talking of your nephews, it's very quiet up there. I hope those boys aren't up to mischief.'

'It wasn't a difficult question, Ally.'

She swallowed. 'Not for you, maybe.'

He looked at her a moment longer, then heaved a sigh and headed back to the kitchen.

Gently Alison rearranged the twisted ribbon around the bear's neck. One carelessly dropped toy. That was all it had taken to spark the chain of events that had led to the loss of her son. If only her husband hadn't had such a relaxed approach to tidiness. If only . . .

She caught herself. She'd been unable to prevent Ben's accident but she *could* make sure this furry little fellow wasn't the cause of another one. With a wistful sigh, she gave the ribbon one final stroke. Then she pushed the bear under the hall table with the rest of the toys, and followed Ross into the kitchen.

Footsteps clattered behind her. 'Uncle Ross! I put it in here!' Luke shouted, brandishing a large biscuit tin. 'But I don't know which one is Ally's.'

Ross beckoned the boys into the kitchen and tipped the keys on to the table.

He stepped back to make room for Ally.

'Any of these look familiar?'

Her hand reached for the keys. Just as Ross's did too.

Their fingers touched for an instant before Alison quickly pulled back.

'A couple of hundred, at a quick guess,' she managed to say with perfect composure.

'Hmmm. That's what I was afraid of.'

Ross swept the keys back into the tin,

then pushed it into a high cupboard.

'It looks like I'll have to take a crowbar to that boarded-up window after all.'

He turned to face the boys.

'I'm off to get some tools out of the garage, then I'll be around at Ally's house for a while. Be good for her while I'm away.'

'You're leaving me to look after them?'

'I don't see any alternative, do you?'

'They could go with you. They caused the problem. Helping you would be a good way to make amends.'

'Good idea. They can finish the washing-up.'

'That's not what I — '

He opened the door. 'Back soon.'

Mark waited for the door to click shut, then flashed Alison a tentative smile. 'I reckon Uncle Ross was only kidding about the washing-up. Why don't me and Luke go and play upstairs?'

It was a tempting offer, but no way to

repay Ross's favour. He'd probably be gone half an hour at the most. Surely she could cope with that?

She took a deep breath and snatched an apron off a hook behind the kitchen door.

'Nice try, Mark.'

Before he'd realised what was happening, she'd looped the apron over his head and positioned a chair by the sink. 'Climb up. You're going to wash. And, Luke . . . ' She rummaged in a drawer for a clean tea towel. 'You can dry.'

'But there are loads!'

Alison smiled to herself. She'd met little boys like this before.

'Losing my spare key has caused your uncle extra work, so you have to do something to make up for it. How about I help you get the kitchen clean and tidy as a nice surprise for when he comes back?'

The boys seemed satisfied with this arrangement, so Alison found a big plastic sack and set to work collecting the rubbish.

'Hey, Uncle Ross wants those!' Luke shouted, when Alison scooped an assortment of flyers from the top of the freezer. 'He'll be cross if you throw them away.'

Surely not? Alison skimmed through them. Two lots of cheap car insurance, this week's supermarket offers, and what was this? *Flirtations . . . a new exciting dating agency. Sign up now for special introductory terms.*

Why on earth had Ross kept this? Surely he had more than enough to occupy his time looking after the boys?

She was still puzzling over the leaflet when the phone rang at the opposite end of the kitchen.

'I'll get it!' Mark scrambled off his chair.

Luke pulled him back. 'No, it's my turn. Ally — tell him!'

By the time Alison had convinced them that she should take the call, the answering machine had kicked in.

'Hi, Ross,' came a chirpy female voice, 'just to let you know that I have

Susanna lined up for you for tomorrow night. It's my guess you'll fall in love with her. But if not, Gemma is waiting in the wings. She's a little older, but I promise you that your kids will love her. Phone when you get this message, and I'll arrange times to suit. Bye-ee!'

Alison's stomach knotted. So Ross had signed with the dating agency already. He must be in a hurry to find a mother for his boys. No wonder he'd been so keen for her to get to know them. He'd realised she had the right skills for the job and couldn't wait to recruit her.

And those kisses, so warm and tender that she'd almost melted into a puddle? Wasn't it obvious? He'd feigned an attraction solely to lure her into the role. With a competent mother at the helm, his discipline problems would vanish, along with Claire Samuels' chances of gaining custody.

Struggling for calm, Alison turned back to the boys, hoping they hadn't overheard the message.

She needn't have worried. They were too busy rummaging through the bin. Alarm darted through her. 'What are you looking for?'

The boys exchanged guilty glances. 'The left-over pizza,' Luke said in a small, contrite voice. 'We're too hungry to wait for breakfast.'

Alison drew a breath between her teeth. To cap it all, their uncle wasn't feeding them properly. Could things get any worse?

* * *

Ross paused outside the kitchen door and took a long, slow sniff. What was that smell? Not their usual breakfast cereal, that was for sure. More like bacon and eggs.

He pushed open the door to see — wonder of wonders — Alison standing at the cooker, tipping the contents of the frying pan on to a serving plate, while Mark and Luke, seated at the table behind her, tucked into some scrambled egg concoction as if all their birthdays had come at once.

This is what family life should be like. Everyone sitting around a table sharing a meal with happy, relaxed expressions on their faces.

'Looks like I timed this just right.'

Alison responded with a frown.

Surely she wasn't still sulking over his hasty exit?

'Sorry to be so long,' he said, sliding the toolbox under the kitchen table. 'But you seem to have managed without me. Why don't you sit down and have some breakfast yourself? It's not fair you doing all this cooking without a reward.'

'I did it because the boys were hungry.'

After their huge supper?

'Oh, they're always hungry.'

'Did you get my keys?'

He took them out of his jogging pants pocket and tossed them on to the table.

'Come on, Ally, stay for a while. The

kids'll be disappointed if you go home now.'

And so would he, he realised with a jolt. He'd seen a softer side to her over the last few hours, and an unexpected spark of playfulness that could almost be construed as flirting. His heart felt lighter than it had in months.

Mark pulled out a chair. 'Hey, Ally, there's a spare place next to me. And before you sit down . . . can I have some more eggy bread?'

Ross blinked. Where did they put it all?

'Not until your brothers have eaten theirs. Nip upstairs and wake them.' In their haste the boys almost toppled the empty chair.

'Hey, slow down,' Alison called after them, her voice threaded with amusement. 'There'll still be plenty left by the time you get back.'

She stooped to push the plate into the warming drawer and when she turned back to Ross her smile was still in place.

His spirits soared. This was better than he'd hoped.

'I knew you'd take to the kids once you got to know them'

She smile morphed into a frown.

'That's why you left them with me, wasn't it? Never mind that I was uncomfortable with the idea. You just had to put your theory to the test.'

What could he say? Nothing for it but to own up. He sent her his most charming smile.

'Guilty as charged. But it worked, didn't it? You seemed to be getting on pretty well.'

She stiffened.

'They're nice kids, but that's as far as it goes. I don't want kids in my life. Not now. Not ever. So don't think you can change my mind about helping you out with them, because you can't.'

This didn't add up. He folded his arms and affected a thoughtful look.

'One thing puzzles me. Why would a single woman choose to live in such an enormous house if she was intending to spend the whole of her life alone?'

She cast him a pitying look. 'I didn't choose it. It chose me — I inherited it from my grandmother.'

'So, you moved in alone?'

'What's with all the questions?' She picked up her keys and turned them over in her palm. 'I had a husband I loved and then I lost him'

Her husband had died? Suddenly everything fell into place. She was not only grieving for the man she loved but had probably convinced herself that no-one could ever replace him. That her chances of becoming a mother had died along with him.

No wonder she was so anti-children. She'd missed the maternal boat and they were a constant reminder of the one thing she would never have.

He placed his hand on her shoulder. 'How long ago?'

'Three years.'

She'd lived here on her own since then? Looking backwards instead of forwards to the future?

'Alison, I'm sorry. I didn't — '

The telephone's strident ring cut off the rest of his answer.

He ignored it. How could he convince this gorgeous creature that she had a future to look forward to?

She shrugged away his hand. 'Aren't you going to answer that?'

'No.'

'I think you ought to.'

She was right. The phone's persistent ring made it impossible to talk. With a heavy sigh he turned and lifted the receiver.

'Ross Anderson, here. How can I help you?'

'Hello, Mr Anderson,' came a woman's fraught voice. 'I live in the cottage across the road. Did you know that your boys are leaning out of an upstairs window, tossing rubbish on to your conservatory roof?'

No, he didn't! And he didn't want Alison to know, either. She'd have a field day with this. Why hadn't he thought to fit window locks? He raked a hand through his hair and avoided her gaze.

'Er, right . . . great of you to call.' He forced his features into a delighted smile. 'Can't talk now, for obvious reasons. But I'll ring you back once I've sorted out — '

'Don't end your call on account of me,' Alison's clipped voice cut in. 'I'm about to go. Thanks for letting me stay over. I'll wash the nightshirt and hand it back later.'

'Alison, wait — ' He dropped the phone into its cradle. 'I've been so wrapped up in my own problems that it never occurred to me that you might have lost your husband. I'm sorry if I've been insensitive. If you ever want to talk about it — '

She didn't let him finish. 'He didn't die, Ross,' she whispered, a catch in her voice. 'He walked out of our marriage because I refused to have a baby. That's how determined I am to keep children out of my life. Now will you please let the matter drop?'

★ ★ ★

Her words rang in his head as he raced up the stairs. That was it, then. Over before it had started. No way was he going to make the mistake of falling for another woman who couldn't love his kids. After all, his ex-fiancée had dumped him right after he'd taken on his ready-made family.

When he reached the bedroom, Mark, Luke and Mattie were standing on the bed to crowd around the open window, while a frustrated Jon struggled to elbow his way on to the sill. Time for some fast action.

'Move away from there, now!'

Startled, they wheeled round and plunked themselves down on the bed, their faces all pictures of guilt.

'Now, would someone like to tell me what's going on?'

'Nothing.' Mark thrust his hands behind his back.

Ross heaved an exasperated sigh. 'What have you got there?'

'Just some eggy bread.'

And this was the boy who'd asked Alison for seconds.

'Well, Mark, would you care to explain why you were dropping your eggy bread out of the window?'

'It's for the cat.'

Cat? Out there? Surely they were pulling his leg?

He climbed on to the bed to take a look for himself. At first all he could see was a tangle of ivy covering the conservatory roof. Then, in the midst of it, he spotted a big fat pumpkin of an orange cat, dozing in the morning sun.

Guilt niggled. So Alison's missing cat wasn't just an excuse to get into his garden and spy on him!

He turned back to the boys.

'How long has it been out there?'

Luke pulled a stash of eggy bread from beneath his pyjama top.

'Only a couple of days. He was scared at first, but now he comes for food. His favourite is pepperoni pizza.'

And chicken drumsticks too, judging

by the debris littering the roof.

'And all this time poor Ally has been looking for her cat. Why on earth didn't you tell me about this?'

'We thought you might be cross.'

'Why should I be cross? It wasn't your fault he went up there, was it?'

No answer. Uh-oh . . .

Ross expelled a sigh. 'OK. What did you do?'

Mark bit his lip. 'I didn't mean to. I was squirting Luke with the hose pipe . . . and the cat sort of got in the way.'

'And?'

'And it got really wet and . . . and then Luke shouted and . . . I think we might have scared it on to the roof.'

'You still should have told me.'

'Luke said that if we told you, you wouldn't let us keep him.'

Ross held on to his patience.

'Too right. First, we can't take anything bigger than a goldfish back to our London flat. And second, Luke, you've no business keeping something that isn't yours. Tiddles here has a perfectly good home with Ally.'

Luke looked affronted. 'Mattie said it was a stray.'

Whoops. Ross could hardly blame the kid for that. It wasn't as if they'd known Alison's cat was missing or even that she owned one. He had to take some of the blame for this.

He closed the window and moved off the bed. 'Then Mattie got it wrong. Now, I want you to go downstairs and finish your breakfasts while I figure out how to get this furball off the roof.'

'He won't come in the window. He's too scared.'

'Don't worry, Luke, I'll get a ladder. Now, downstairs, all of you — oh, and it might be a good idea not to tell Ally you stole her cat. What she doesn't know won't hurt her.'

★　★　★

Back in her own home and dressed in her work clothes again, Alison pulled open the washing machine door and

119

tossed in the borrowed nightshirt. She'd wait until Ross's cousin came back before returning it. She wouldn't want him to mistake obligation for interest; although after the parting shot she'd delivered he'd have to be very thick skinned not to have got the message. She doubted he'd want her anywhere near those boys from now on.

Which was exactly what she'd intended. There'd be no more cosy breakfasts, battles with midnight monsters . . . and certainly no more kisses.

And that, she decided as she set the washing machine in motion, was the last time she would think about him or his nephews.

Then as she opened the back door to replace the previous night's cat food, a streak of orange fur shot through the gap. What the . . . Pusskins?

Tail twitching, back stiffened, Pusskins skulked under the table.

Thank goodness he was back! But this wasn't like him. Something must have scared him. Alison slid the saucer of food towards him, then walked back to the door to take a look outside.

'Ally! Ally!' Mark and Luke were running up her path, their faces contorted in panic.

Heart sinking, she ran towards them. 'What happened? Did my cat scratch you?'

Mark shook his head. 'It's . . . Uncle Ross.' The boy could scarcely get his words out.

'Come quick!' Luke grabbed her arm. 'He was on the conservatory roof and he fell off his ladder. And now he won't wake up.'

Oh, please don't let him be dead! Without another thought, she bolted across the grass and down the side of the cottage next door. Ross was sprawled on the ground beside the dilapidated ivy-clad conservatory with Mattie and Jon, both white-faced, crouched at his side.

'Ross?' she whispered, crouching down beside them.

This couldn't be happening. Only a

short while ago they'd been laughing, teasing, kissing. Ross was vital and fun. Seeing him lying there, so hurt and vulnerable, twisted her heart.

'Ross . . . ' — panic laced her words — 'Ross . . . can you hear me?'

His eyelids flickered.

'Ally?' A tiny smile lit his face. 'Give me a minute to get my bearings and then I'll be back on my feet.'

His voice sounded groggy. Distant.

He struggled to haul himself into a sitting position. Then gave a loud gasp.

'I think I might have sprained my ankle,' he panted. 'I'll be all right in a bit.'

Who was he kidding? Anyone could see the man was in dreadful pain.

'Mattie, does your uncle have a mobile phone?'

A nod.

'Would you run and get it, please?'

Mattie got to his feet, then paused, looking stricken. 'I can't. Jon dropped it down the toilet. Uncle Ross is waiting for it to dry out.'

'In that case . . . ' She tried to keep her voice matter-of-fact. 'I want you to run back through the fence to my kitchen and bring me my black leather handbag off the kitchen table. Jon, you go too, and help him find it. Then, if you can manage it, drop the latch on your way out.'

'What about me and Mark?' Luke demanded with a squawk of indignation. 'What can we do?'

'I need you to fetch your house keys, lock the back door, then stand at the front gate and watch for the ambulance. I'll ring for it the minute Mattie brings my bag, so you shouldn't have to wait very long.'

As the boys ran to do Alison's bidding, Ross motioned for her to help him off with his shoe. 'I'm sure it's just a sprain. Don't call an amb — ' He broke off, his face contorted with pain.

'Don't be ridiculous, Ross,' she said, removing the shoe as gently as she could. 'You obviously need to go to hospital.'

'No — wait.' Biting his lip he leaned forward to unzip the leg of his jogging pants, then tentatively fingered his swelling ankle. 'If you could get someone to help me into the house and sort out a cold compress, I'll be OK in an hour or two. There's no way I'm leaving the boys. What if I need to be kept in?'

'If you're worried about finding someone to look after them, then I'm sure the neighbours will pitch in to help.'

'I can't leave them with strangers,' he said, looking at her appealingly.

This was crazy. Did he really imagine, after all she'd told him, that she was about to volunteer? She fixed him with a stern look. 'Then your options have just run out.'

He cast her a sideways glance. 'The kids could come to the hospital with me if you bundled them into my car and followed behind the ambulance.'

She shook her head. 'That's not much of a solution. What if the doctors do keep you in?'

'We'll worry about that if and when it happens, but for now it's important we stay together.' His expression was pleading. 'Come on, Ally, you saw the boys' faces. If I leave them now, they'll convince themselves I'm not coming back. That I've gone for ever, just like their parents.'

Alison bit back a sigh. And the longer he was away, the more scared and anxious they would become. How could she put them through that?

House Guests For Alison

The boys were so quiet on the way to the hospital that even the sight of a carnival in the grounds hardly raised a comment. It wasn't until they were allowed into the treatment bay to see Ross that their vitality returned.

Matt greeted him with a high five. 'How are you feeling, Uncle Ross?'

'With my hands, the same as I always do!'

Standing apart from the boys, shoulder leaned against the wall, Alison shook her head as she surveyed the scene. Ross lay on a trolley, his ankle discoloured and swollen, yet he could still find it in himself to joke.

'Thanks for bringing them, Alison.' His eyes met her gaze over the boys' heads. 'I really appreciate it.'

'Like I had any choice.' She softened her words with a laugh but the meaning couldn't have been clearer. He'd railroaded her into this and she did *not* want to be involved. 'How's the pain now?'

The laughter left his eyes. 'It's settled to a dull roar.'

Still excruciating, then. Yet despite his discomfort, he teased and wise-cracked until he convinced the boys that nothing was seriously amiss.

This man's experience with children might be a little thin but he had the knack of keeping them happy. Her heart warmed at the thought. What would it be like to be part of such a family? To live together? Laugh together? Love together?

For a fleeting moment she imagined waking in his warm embrace. His lips pressing kisses against her tangled hair.

She dragged her mind back to order.

If and when she entered into another relationship, it wouldn't be with a man who had children, and certainly not with one who only wanted her for her childcare skills.

Her stomach twisted. What had happened to her? Two days ago she would never have considered the possibility of another relationship. What was this man doing to her?

'So what do you think?'

'Pardon?' She brushed away her vague yearnings and met Ross's gaze.

He gave her a teasing smile.

'Earth to Ally. I asked if you'd mind taking the kids to the snack bar while I'm in X-ray?'

He had a lovely smile. It started in his eyes, brightening them to a mischievous gleam, before piercing a tiny dimple in his left cheek.

'Y — yes, of course I'll take them.'

She forced herself not to look at the dimple.

Jon moved to her side and thrust his tiny hand into hers.

'Will Uncle Ross still be here when we get back?'

Alison glanced down into his wide, anxious eyes. Poor little thing. He wasn't sure of anything any more.

She forced a smile into her voice. 'Of course he will. He's only having his photograph taken.'

She shifted her gaze to his brothers and saw the same uncertainty in their eyes. The thought of the four boys spending the next few hours sitting in the hospital, waiting and wondering, brought a lump to her throat.

'Then, after your snack, maybe you'd like to go to the hospital carnival?'

'Yeees!'

Catching the look of relief in Ross's eyes, she felt her throat tighten again. Watching over his nephews while he was being X-rayed was the least she could do. Anything less would be totally selfish.

'Come on then,' she said, 'there'll be a queue a mile long if we don't hurry up.'

Mattie led the way, his shoulders slumped. 'I wish Uncle Ross was coming with us.'

Me too. The thought came unbidden. Quickly she squashed it and hurried not just from the room but from the treacherous thoughts slipping into her mind, and from the man who caused them.

* * *

When they returned to the hospital, the boys did as she suggested and played with the toys in the waiting area, too tired to make a fuss.

Alison gave them a few minutes to settle. Then, taking advantage of a middle-aged couple's offer to keep an eye on them, she slipped into the treatment area to check up on Ross.

'He's just back from the plaster room,' the nurse told her, pulling aside the curtain surrounding the trolley. 'He has a break just above his ankle and a touch of concussion, so we're debating whether to keep him in overnight.'

'I can't stay,' Ross said, the minute the nurse was out of earshot. 'I've promised the kids that I'm coming home. I have to get out of here today.'

Easy enough said. But what about the practicalities?

'So what are your plans?'

'I need someone to stay overnight. It's standard procedure when a patient has concussion. If I can guarantee that, then they'll let me out.'

He definitely hadn't thought this through. Alison didn't want to be the one to burst his bubble, but she had to make him see that there was no easy answer to this. And absolutely no chance she would volunteer.

'I'm sure one of the neighbours would step in if I asked them,' she told him, 'but that still leaves the problem of the next day and the days after that. You're in no fit state to look after the boys on your own. You need long-term help.'

He nodded towards a pair of crutches propped against the wall. 'I'll be OK once I've mastered those.'

That smile again. With the power to knock her sideways.

'Ross, the boys' behaviour won't

miraculously improve just because you need it to. In fact, it'll probably get a whole lot worse when they realise you're at a disadvantage.'

'We'll see.'

Was there no limit to his optimism?

'The doctors won't let you out until they're sure you can cope, and unless you organise someone to look after the boys, social services could whisk them into care.'

There was a long, drawn-out silence.

'So what do I do?'

'You've mentioned the boys' maternal grandmother?' she suggested, feeling guilty about concealing the fact that she'd actually met Claire Samuels, but she didn't want to make the relationship between Ross and Mrs Samuels even worse than it already was.

'No way! She'd just use my incapacity against me and try to gain custody of the boys!'

'So how about paying for help? One of my clients runs an agency offering help in a crisis. Child-minding, dog-sitting, domestic help. If I contact her, she'll probably get a nanny to you within the hour. A housekeeper too, if you need one.'

He considered a moment, then frowned and shook his head.

It was a perfectly good offer. What was holding him back?

'Look, if it's a question of money,' she said softly, 'the social services are bound to run some kind of home care service. You've got to have someone to help you. You can't possibly manage alone.'

His frown deepened. 'I . . . ' His words tailed off.

'You don't want any kind of home care scheme do you?'

He gave a long sigh. Then he grinned and shot her a sideways glance.

'Been there, done that, got the T-shirt . . . and wore it out, long since. Believe me, it's not an option.'

'Are you going to tell me why?'

He drew a fractured breath. 'When the boys lost their parents I was living overseas. I flew back to London, gave up my flat, and moved into the family home. Then, after a couple of weeks, I found myself a job and left the kids in the very capable hands of their nanny, who'd been working for the family for a couple of years by that time.'

'A sensible idea. So what was the problem?'

'Everything was fine until the nanny retired and I couldn't find anyone to match her. Nannies came and went, the kids' behaviour got more and more out of control, and then to cap it all, the housekeeper left.'

'Because of the boys?'

'Yep. In the end I was relying on a succession of agency workers, each averaging less than a week in the job before they threw up their hands in despair and left.'

'And that was when you decided to come here?'

'Not quite.' He absently fingered the edge of his T-shirt. 'I went to see their former nanny hoping to lure her out of

134

retirement, but she'd made plans to join her sister in Australia so that was the end of that. She'd been my last hope. The journey wasn't completely wasted, though. She explained that the boys needed constancy. That I needed to cut back my work hours and bond with them. That their behaviour wouldn't change until I did.'

She lifted an eyebrow at him. 'Wise woman.'

'That's what I figured. When my cousin offered me her cottage I realised that a few months away on neutral territory was the fresh start we needed. I told myself that if I steered clear of hired help and gave the boys my un-divided attention, our problems would disappear.' He gave a dejected sigh. 'Hiring agency workers at this stage would throw us right back to square one. If you think the kids are a handful now, you should have seen them before.' Then, clearly realising that he'd said too much, he added, 'But this holiday will still turn things around. My broken ankle is only a temporary glitch.'

She studied the taut lines of his face. Ross might sound optimistic but his expression told a different story. He'd reached the end of his tether. He needed someone responsible to step in and take control of the situation.

'If you're dead set against agency workers, and you're not wanting to give the children's maternal grandmother an excuse to step in and take over, then what about any other relations?'

'My parents dote on the kids and would do anything for them.' He sighed again. 'But they live miles away. It'd take them hours to get here.'

'They'd come, though?'

'Oh, yes.' He considered a moment, then shook his head. 'It wouldn't be fair to ask them. They're both retired. Looking after the boys would be too much of a strain. My father's already had one heart attack. I wouldn't want to cause another.'

Alison squelched a growing feeling of helplessness. So far he'd shot down every possibility.

'So, if we forget about your parents for the moment, that leaves you with two clear options. The agency or the boys' grandmother. Which is it to be?'

His eyes caught hers and held them.

The way he looked at her brought a sudden clanging of alarm bells. No! He couldn't expect her to step in. Not after everything she'd told him.

'I'm sorry, Ross, but you know how I feel about children. I really can't help you here.'

He leaned back on his pillows and closed his eyes. 'No, I'm the one who should be sorry. Desperation makes people behave irrationally sometimes. Forget I even asked.'

As her eyes travelled over his ashen complexion, she felt a rush of sympathy. Even at his lowest ebb, Ross was determined to care for the boys himself. Their grandmother might love them but Ross clearly did too. Maybe he wasn't the blasé parent she'd been led to believe.

A swish of curtains interrupted her thoughts. A doctor stepped into the cubicle, followed by Mark and Luke.

'I found these two wandering around outside. They'd like to know when their uncle is coming home.'

Ross's tight expression relaxed into a smile. 'This afternoon, I hope.' He nodded towards Alison. 'This is my next-door neighbour. We're just discussing what help I'll need.'

The doctor adjusted his glasses and peered at Ross's ankle.

'Did the nurse explain that we've given you a temporary cast so you can leave on crutches? You won't be able to put any weight on the foot. At least, not until you get a walking cast.'

'But I can leave today?'

'Provided you have someone with you for the next twenty-four hours, and help in the house for the next few weeks.' He lifted Ross's notes from the end of the trolley. 'And from now on, if you spot any more cats on your roof, please call the fire brigade. Or better

138

still, wait for the crafty little creatures to climb down. They all manage it sooner or later.'

Luke gave a chortle. 'This one couldn't. It was too fat and too scared. That's why Uncle Ross had to go up his ladder.'

Mark dealt his brother a sharp dig in the ribs. 'Shhh! Uncle Ross said to keep quiet about that!'

Alison's mind raced. 'That was my cat, wasn't it?' she said slowly. 'You fell rescuing Pusskins.'

'Pusskins?' Ross shot her a bemused grin. 'That big orange bruiser couldn't possibly have such an innocuous name as Pusskins. Basher or Slasher, maybe. But Pusskins — never!'

So Ross had broken his ankle rescuing Pusskins and, like a true hero, he'd kept the whole thing quiet. How thoughtful. How brave. How . . . chivalrous.

Tears pricked her eyes. Nobody had done anything like that for her before. Ross was a man in a million.

'Thank you so much,' she said in a choked voice.

The doctor cleared his throat and looked up from his notes.

'So, Mr Anderson, is there someone who can stay with you overnight?'

Ross heaved a long-suffering sigh.

'No.'

'Someone to care for the children if you're discharged tomorrow?'

'No.'

Alison took a deep breath. She wasn't normally the type to make rash decisions, but she couldn't leave Ross in the lurch. Not when her cat had caused the whole sorry predicament.

'Yes.'

The doctor looked from Ross to Alison

'We seem to have a slight discrepancy here.'

Alison cleared her throat.

'Yes,' she repeated, meeting Ross's stunned gaze. 'To both questions.'

'Alison . . . ' Ross's voice held a warning note. 'We haven't agreed anything yet. I meant what I said about bringing in strangers.'

'I know.' She turned to the doctor. 'The family will stay with me until Mr Anderson is well enough to look after the boys himself.'

The family stared at her in wide-eyed astonishment.

Warm with embarrassment, Alison added, 'Er — if that's all right with everyone?'

'I'm sure it is.' The doctor tucked the notes under his arm. 'Just remember that if there's any nausea or dizziness he'll need to come straight back. Now, if you'll excuse me, I'll ask the nurse to find you a leaflet listing other symptoms you'll need to watch out for.'

★   ★   ★

It was all Ross could do to find his voice. Despite Alison's aversion to kids, she'd invited them into her home. Not just for today but the next few weeks. And him as well!

141

'Thank you,' he said at last, in a hoarse voice.

She avoided his gaze.

'It's the least I can do after what my cat has put you through.'

Heck. Now he felt like a king-sized rat. He was no hero and should tell her so right away — explain that the kids had stolen her cat, and that he'd tried to cover their crime by sneaking the little blighter back to her garden.

But what if she withdrew her offer? He had no alternative but to keep quiet.

'You won't regret this, I promise.'

I probably will, her expression said.

'The offer comes with a few conditions.'

'Fire away.'

She squared her shoulders.

'I need peace and quiet to work. So, during the day, I want you to hand the boys over to professionals. Not nannies or childminders,' she added, when she saw his frown. 'Another client of mine runs a summer play scheme at the school. If the boys joined, they'd be in a safe environment with plenty to keep them occupied.'

He had no argument with that. If he were honest, the constant pressure of having them twenty-four hours a day was beginning to tell on him, although he'd never admit that to anyone.

He shifted his attention to the other two sombre faces at the end of his trolley. 'Did you hear that, kids? Ally's sorted out a great daytime club for you. What's the betting you'll get to play football?'

'Yeees!' Mark and Luke exchanged high fives.

Ross grinned and reached for his crutches.

'Now, go fetch your brothers. Then we can all go home.'

The relief on their faces banished any remaining feelings of guilt he harboured. Without Alison's offer, the kids would suffer. There was nothing so certain as that. He'd think of some way to make it up to her, and in the meantime, he'd make sure his family wasn't a burden.

'Thanks again, Alison,' he said, once the boys had left the cubicle. 'I'll do my best to keep them out of your hair.'

'You'd better.'

Ross rubbed his forefinger and thumb against his temples. Although her words were said with a smile, her eyes held a determined gleam. How would a woman who'd no time for children cope with four lively boys constantly under her feet?

The thought sobered him. Thankfully Alison had done a good job of hiding her feelings from the boys so far, and he'd no cause to suppose that would change. If they all trod carefully and no-one became emotionally involved, there was no reason why this arrangement couldn't work.

★ ★ ★

While Alison and the boys went to collect the car from the car park, they left Ross sitting on a bench outside the hospital entrance.

When they returned, a striking brunette was sitting beside him, her hand resting possessively on his arm. The woman wore a deep blue nurse's uniform — the colour setting off to perfection her sun-kissed complexion and luxurious swathe of rich, dark hair.

Who on earth was she? And how did she know Ross?

Resisting the urge to stare, Alison climbed out of the car and walked round to open the front passenger door as quietly and carefully as she could. The boys had all fallen fast asleep as soon as they'd got into the back of the car, and she didn't want to disturb them.

'Alison — ' Ross eased himself to his feet and swung towards her, the woman following at his side. 'I'd like you to meet Maria, a friend of mine from London. She's just started work on the children's ward here.'

'Pleased to meet you, Maria.' Alison stepped forward and offered what she hoped was a friendly smile. 'And are you settling in to your new job OK?'

Maria gave an answering smile, two tiny dimples piercing her smooth, bronze cheeks. 'Oh yes. And I lived here in this area until I was eighteen, so I'm enjoying catching up with old friends.' She slanted Ross a look from under her lashes. 'And some not so old ones as well. It's a great surprise to bump into Ross like this!'

Alison didn't hear Ross's reply but Maria's manner was almost flirtatious. Was she hoping for more than friendship from him? The thought of him kissing Maria as he'd kissed her brought a strange tightening to the centre of Ally's chest.

'Ross tells me you're his neighbour?' Maria continued, shooting Alison an appraising look. 'And that he's railroaded you into looking after him and those four lively nephews of his until he's fit again? I've never met them but I understand they're quite a handful. Are they in the car?'

'Yes, but they're fast asleep just now, and he didn't actually railroad me. I volunteered.'

'Hey, that's brave, considering they've seen off a truckload of nannies and one long-term fiancée.'

'Maria, that's way too much information,' interrupted Ross, a shadow crossing his face, 'I'll be lucky if Alison doesn't change her mind after that.'

'Sorry, Alison. I was only joking.'

'It's all right. I knew about the nannies. But Ross has kept very quiet about the fiancée. What's the story there?'

Maria gave a little shrug. 'I don't know. He was just about to tell me when you came along.'

'What's to tell?' A brief look of pain crossed Ross's face. 'It turned out that Lauren wasn't the kind of woman to take on someone else's kids. When she couldn't persuade me to shunt them off to boarding school, she broke off the engagement.'

Alison blinked at the hurt in his tone.

Had the experience left him so cynical that he was prepared to make a play for any woman who had the childcare skills he needed?

Maria clutched his arm. 'Oh, Ross, I'm so sorry. That must have been a huge blow.' She peeped at him from under her lashes. 'But don't let it put you off getting involved again. I bet there are tons of women out there who'd jump at the chance to be your wife — ready-made family or not.'

'If only I had the time to meet them,' he said in a wry tone.

Maria shot Ross another dimpled smile. 'Maybe you already have.'

There was a momentary silence. 'Could be.'

Maria smoothed her dress. 'Listen, if ever you need anyone to take the boys off your hands for an hour or two, let me know. I'm free most evenings and I love young children.'

Ross grinned. 'You might change your mind once you get to know my bubbling brood.'

'I doubt it.' She looked across at the car. 'I haven't met a kid yet I didn't like, or one I couldn't get along with.'

He looked more than interested. 'In which case, thank you for the offer.'

'That's settled then.' Maria fished around in her bag and produced a pen and a scrap of paper. 'Here's my number.' She scribbled on the paper then, with a proprietary air, tucked it into Ross's shirt pocket. 'Call me any time. Even if it's only for a chat. We've a lot of catching up to do.'

'Will do.'

With a grin, Ross handed Alison his crutches and swung into the car, while Maria walked back to the hospital entrance.

Alison stared after her. If Ross took up Maria's offer to babysit, she most likely wouldn't be just his babysitter for long. The woman had all the qualities Ross needed in a wife and from the way she looked at him she wouldn't need much persuading to take on that role.

But either way, it was no business of Alison's. Ross was free to have a relationship with whoever he pleased.

★ ★ ★

When Alison parked Ross's car in his driveway, Ross sent Mattie inside to collect toothbrushes, pyjamas, and whatever he could find in the freezer.

Mission accomplished, the family headed to Alison's house where the kids watched cartoons in her living-room while she threw together a hasty spaghetti bolognaise.

So far so good, she thought, as the boys' happy laughter drifted through to the kitchen. Maybe they weren't such a handful after all. Maybe a calm atmosphere was all it took to quieten them down.

But dinner marked the end of the honeymoon period. Mark and Luke scowled at the fresh carrots in their bolognaise sauce and refused to eat, but once they realised Alison wasn't about to rifle through her cupboards looking for alternatives, they stopped grumbling and cleared their plates.

Knowing there was no way the boys would settle to watch more cartoons, Alison searched the living-room sideboard for something to occupy them and eventually unearthed a pack of cards and a tin of buttons.

The next couple of hours saw the boys playing simple card games with their uncle. Alison made everyone a drink, sorted out the sleeping arrangements and then, with the promise of one of Ross's stories to follow, she managed to persuade each boy into a warm, sudsy bath. By eight o'clock they were all in bed.

When she came downstairs, Ross was absorbed in a game of Patience.

'I've given the boys a bedroom each,' she told him, reaching for his empty coffee mug, 'and I'm pleased to report they are all fast asleep.'

His eyes glinted with devilment. 'Is this your way of telling me that I'm bunking in with you?'

Heat rushed into her cheeks. She knew he was teasing so why was she blushing like a schoolgirl?

She grabbed the mug and turned her burning face away from him. 'I'll pretend I didn't hear that. I've made up the bed settee in my sitting-room for you. I thought you'd find it easier than struggling with the stairs.'

'A sofa bed as well as five furnished bedrooms?' He flipped over a card. 'Now why would someone who insists she enjoys living alone cater for so many guests?'

Because she'd once loved having people around her. Loved the arrival of her foster brothers' and sisters' rumble-tumble families — until she'd lost Ben and stopped the invitations.

'My gran liked to entertain,' she said, after a long pause. 'The furniture was a legacy from her. Anything else you'd like to know?'

He played his last card, then gathered up the pack. 'Only what we'll be doing tomorrow. Come and sit down while we talk it over.'

We? He made it sound as though the two of them were a unit. Now was her chance to set a few things straight.

She deliberately avoided the space next to him on the sofa and perched on the edge of the nearby chair.

'What would you normally do on a Sunday?' she asked him.

'Go wherever the mood takes me. Except that tomorrow the kids have a swimming lesson booked.' He gave a wry smile and looked down at his cast. 'I guess my broken ankle has put paid to that.'

'No reason why they should miss their swimming. I could drop them off and pick them up again later. They might not allow Jon to take part without an adult present, but he'd maybe enjoy some individual time with you while I get on with my work.'

'You're a star.'

That smile again. With its capacity to knock her right off course.

'What were your plans for the rest of the day?'

'I thought I'd let the boys play in the garden,' he said with a shrug. 'Doing whatever it is that kids do. Running. Wrestling. Squirting each other with the hosepipe . . . ' His mouth quirked. 'Kicking a football if their grumpy neighbour agrees to give it back.'

'Oh, no. I still have my work to do, and I can't do it in the midst of chaos.'

He raised an eyebrow.

'Then they'll just have to watch TV.'

How long did he think they'd do that before squabbles broke out?

'They'll soon get bored.'

He gave her a patient smile.

'So what's your solution?'

'How about we draw up a schedule of quiet activities and make sure the boys stick to it? Not just for tomorrow, but the whole of your stay.'

The thought of finding himself trapped in a quiet, predictable lifestyle brought Ross out in a cold sweat.

'Quiet? This is planet boy. They don't do quiet.'

'Then they'll have to learn.'

Ross studied the determined glint in her silver-grey eyes. Why did she have this urge to control her surroundings? Did she think something bad would happen if she left a few things to chance?

'And to think I awarded you eight out of ten for spontaneity. I hope you realise your rating has just fallen to zero.'

A smile flickered at the corners of her mouth.

'They can still be spontaneous but in a quieter way. There's no need for perpetual motion. It won't do the boys any harm to discover their more sensitive sides.'

He stifled a groan. She wouldn't be happy until they were threading daisy chains and pirouetting across the lawn.

'Let me get this right. You want to plan every minute of our day from getting up in the morning to going to

155

bed at night — with the emphasis on peace and quiet?'

'That's right. During the week, the boys will get plenty of chances to let off steam at the play centre. And for the time between sessions, we draw up some rules and make a list of suitable activities. What do you say?'

He stared at her in disbelief. Schedules, rules and planners were OK for the workplace, but in the home . . . ?

'Ally, it's great what you're doing for us, and I *am* grateful. But do you have to have quite such a . . . conservative approach?'

She gave him a bright smile.

'In case you hadn't noticed, I'm a pretty conservative type of person.'

Maybe on the surface. But underneath, he wasn't so sure. Would a conservative person have driven away a little boy's nightmares in such an innovative fashion? Or let his uncle chase her around his kitchen in a crazy soap bubble fight? No. She was as capable of having fun as the next person. She just needed a little help realising it.

He met her gaze squarely.

'The kids are supposed to be on holiday. And holidays mean fun. There's no fun in sterile planners and charts.'

Her spine stiffened.

'Maybe that's your problem, Ross,' she said in a tight little voice. 'Raising children is a huge responsibility. If you can't accept that, and you can't bear the thought of their grandmother having control of their lives, then maybe you should think about sending them to boarding school.'

'That's something I'd never agree to,' he said, flinching. 'My parents sent me to boarding school and I never got over the feeling of abandonment, even after my brother joined me there.'

She gave a twisted smile.

'And was your bad behaviour the reason your parents sent you away?'

'Certainly not! We had our moments, but our behaviour was never out of control. In fact, my childhood was really quite idyllic. We grew up on the edge of a small Scottish island with beautiful sandy beaches.' The memory brought a smile. 'In summer we played outside all day, going out in boats almost as soon as we could walk. It was a life of amazing freedom and we were too busy to cause our parents any serious problems.'

'So, why were you sent away?'

'The school closed, and we had to board at a school on a neighbouring island. The new school was too far away to travel daily and the journey across a rough stretch of water often meant missing weekends at home.'

He attempted to inject some lightness into his tone.

'We came home for the holidays, of course, but things were never the same. I still remember the sense of adventure those early years brought and I want that same feeling for my nephews.'

'You think you'll get it here?'

'For a few months maybe, but I couldn't live in this quiet backwater for long. I'd feel life was passing me by. Come winter, I plan to travel and take the boys with me.'

'What about their education?'

He picked up the cards and shuffled them.

'You can't beat the education you get from seeing the world. Childhood passes like sand through a sieve. It shouldn't be spent sitting behind a desk.'

'So you won't be sending them to school?'

'No school. No ties. No hectic city schedules.' He spread the cards across the table and stole a glance at her. 'I want to give those kids a childhood to remember.'

Her eyes were thoughtful.

'No job. No income. How will you manage?'

'I'll get by. It'll be a great adventure, Ally. I can't wait.'

'But at the moment you're in no fit state to go anywhere,' she pointed out. 'So like it or not, you're in for a few weeks of very necessary routine. How about I dig out a wall planner and we draw up that schedule?'

'Do I have a choice?'

An unexpected glimmer of mischief entered her eyes.

'Of course you don't. We'll sort it out tomorrow.'

He sent her one of his most charming smiles.

Like heck they would. Broken ankle or not, he wasn't settling into a life of dull routine for anyone.

Alison's Heartbreak

Silence greeted Alison when she woke the next morning. Good. Maybe she would manage a couple of hours' work before her guests surfaced. After the hectic events of the last twenty-four hours, she badly needed to catch up.

Sunday wasn't a day for seeing clients, so she dressed in a cream cheesecloth shirt and a pair of black jeans and scooped her hair into a casual ponytail.

When she reached under the bed for some sandals, her fingers closed over Claire Samuels' forgotten-about notebook.

She pulled it out, wondering whether it was fair to be keeping a record of her next-door neighbour's unconventional child-rearing methods. It seemed a sneaky and underhand way to behave given that Ross and the boys were now under her roof and that she could see for herself how much the children were loved by their uncle.

But writing down the events of the past few days, and her feelings about all that had happened, might help her to get her thoughts in order — even though she had no real intention of passing the notebook back to the boys' grandmother.

Once she began writing she couldn't stop. Her hand sped over the pages, spilling out all her fears and frustrations until the sound of childish laughter outside her bedroom door brought her outpourings to a halt.

With a sigh, she snapped the book closed, pushed it back under her bed, and opened her door just in time to see a giggling Luke stuffing a wet flannel down Mark's pyjama top. Stifling a smile, she confiscated the flannel, affected a stern expression, and dispatched them to get dressed.

She had to get Ross to agree to some rules. The sooner the children understood the boundaries, the better. It was the only way this arrangement could work.

It was mid-morning before she had a chance to broach the subject again. She'd dropped the boys off at their swimming lesson, and was busy writing a shopping list when Ross hopped into the kitchen.

'So this is where you're hiding?'

'I'm not hiding. I'm making a list of what we'll need from the supermarket before — '

'Jon wakes up and breaks your concentration.' He gave a knowing smile. 'Very wise, and in the meantime how about a coffee? I'll make it if you'll carry the mugs to the table?'

His words brought an answering smile. She must have caught him in a co-operative mood.

'That sounds like a good division of labour.'

He perched on the edge of the table and propped his crutches against a vacant chair.

'I'm more than happy to do my

share. Just tell me what you need me to do.'

'How about I write it on a planner?'

He folded his arms, amusement lighting his eyes.

'How about you just tell me?'

So he was still resisting her planner, and the rules, too. Never mind. She would find a way to bring the topic back into the conversation. She wasn't giving up on this.

'I could do with some help with the shopping.'

His eyes twinkled. 'I suppose I could carry the basket between my teeth.'

She smiled and pushed a strand of hair away from her forehead.

'With any luck that won't be necessary. I've an account with the big supermarket in town, but they need two days' notice to organise a delivery. Could you place an on-line order while I'm away at the local store, stocking up with enough to tide us over?'

'No worries. Let me see what you need.' Ross leaned on one arm and turned the list towards him. 'Just as I thought. There's enough here to feed a small army. I'll set up a new account with my credit card details.'

A sudden flush of heat burned her face. Did he think this was the reason she'd asked him to help? To shame him into picking up the bill? She stared at him, unsure what to say. Her words had simply been a lead-in to a discussion on splitting the chores and drawing up an action plan.

'You can't do that. You're my guests — I invited you.'

'And you're a single woman struggling to build a business. There's no way you'll stretch to five hungry guests. The food is on me. It's the least I can do.'

Her cheeks heated again. He was right. She couldn't afford to feed them. But she couldn't let him pay for her food, too. She wasn't part of the family. Just a neighbour repaying the favour of having her cat rescued, and she wanted to keep it that way. She'd take care of the bill for this morning's shopping. That should help even things out.

He laughed at her hesitation. 'Hey, I'm not asking you to marry me. Just offering to pay my way.'

Her heart lurched as he grinned again. 'I never imagined . . . '

'I was teasing.'

Of course he was. She willed her racing heart to slow down. She had to get out of here. Put some distance between them. She neither liked nor understood the direction her thoughts were taking.

She pushed back her chair and glanced at the clock. 'Eleven o'clock already?' She gave a light laugh. 'I'd better skip that coffee or I won't have time to shop before I collect the boys.'

He continued to look at her, a soft smile curving his mouth. 'What are you running from, Ally? Me — or my situation?'

'W-what do you mean?'

He leaned closer. 'If I didn't have the boys, would you still run?'

As she looked into the searching brown eyes, her heart raced again. Why did his question evoke such . . . panic?

'If you didn't have the boys . . . ' she managed, with an awkward little laugh, 'then . . . '

'Go on . . . '

There was no way she could avoid the truth. Her response to yesterday's kisses had told him he didn't repulse her. And his question was hypothetical — there was no way he would give up the boys. And no way would she want him to.

'And if you were the type of man who didn't want children, ever . . . '

' . . . so you're definitely not keen on kids?' he finished for her.

'You find that hard to understand, don't you?' she said, desperate to switch the conversation. 'That a woman can be so set on not wanting a family.'

'Not at all. It's hard enough coping with children when you want them. I'd never wish them on someone who didn't. But one thing puzzles me. You must have known how you felt before you married. Surely you and your husband discussed it then?'

She looked down at the table.

'We married young and our plans were vague.'

No need to lie about that. Two or three children for starters then more if they could afford it — what could be more vague than that?

'He pressed me to have a baby when I wasn't ready and didn't know if I ever would be. He couldn't live with that and the marriage ended.'

Ross looked at her silently for a moment.

'Any regrets?'

She toyed with her pen, then slowly she nodded.

'We wanted different things, and because I loved him I gave him the freedom to meet someone else.' The words came out as a whisper. 'He has a new wife now and the baby he yearned for. How could I have denied him that?'

'You never thought of marrying

again?' Ross asked gently. 'Not all men want children. Your husband moved on, so why couldn't you?'

She stared through the window into the warm summer sunshine. How much could she safely tell him?

'Probably because I couldn't find that same feeling with anyone else.' She moistened her dry lips. 'Now I have my work to keep me busy.'

'And you've never felt the need for a diversion?' He leaned closer and caught a stray tendril of her hair. Let it coil around his fingers.

Not until now. She clenched her thumbs tightly under the edge of the table, a warm tingle caressing her spine. How long could she deny the awareness she felt around him? The attraction that danced between them?

He tipped her chin.

Maybe it didn't matter that he was the wrong man for a permanent relationship. Why not enjoy being with him for as long as it lasted, then transfer her newly awakened feelings to someone more suitable? Surely a few kisses couldn't hurt. In a short while he would have the wife he wanted and both of them would move on.

Slowly she raised her face to his.

'Uncle Ross, where are you?' A small voice sounded from the hall.

Ross expelled a breath and hauled himself upright.

'In here, Jon.'

The kitchen door banged open. 'Where are the others?' the small boy demanded, his brows pulled together in an indignant scowl. 'Everyone's gone and left me again!'

'And a good morning to you, too,' Ross said, with a grin. Then, when Jon pushed out his bottom lip, 'They're at their swimming class. Yours doesn't start for a few weeks so we left you to sleep in. Nip back upstairs and get dressed. Then I'll find you some breakfast.'

'Ice cream?' A hopeful look entered the little boy's eyes.

'Ally doesn't have any ice-cream.'

Ross sent her a conspiratorial glance. 'But if you manage to get dressed all by yourself and eat some toast, she might bring some back from the shop.'

'And chocolate sprinkles?'

'I don't see why not.'

'Yes! Ice-cream with chocolate sprinkles. My favourite.' Jon ran to the door with a skip and a whoop.

Ross rubbed his jaw and cast Alison a bemused look.

'I'm not sure who had the upper hand there. But I've a feeling it wasn't me.'

The smile that accompanied his words sparked such a rush of warmth that in that one moment, Alison knew a summer flirtation with this man could never be enough. She would always want more. And that 'more' involved loving his children, a risk she couldn't afford to take.

She snatched up her list. 'Time I wasn't here.'

'Before you go . . . ' Ross pulled a wallet out of his back pocket and dropped a credit card on the table. 'Put everything on my plastic. Give me your hand.'

'What?'

Taking his weight on one elbow, he leaned across the table. 'Your hand,' he repeated, a wicked glint in his eyes.

Before she could pull away, warm, strong fingers captured hers and pulled them against his chest.

She took a sharp breath. 'W-what are you doing?'

'Patience, Alison.' With his free hand, he pushed up the sleeve of her sweatshirt, the gentle pressure of his fingers sending tiny ripples of pleasure dancing along her arm and up her neck.

Heat swept into her cheeks. 'I don't really . . . '

He responded by grabbing her pen and running the delicate tip along the inside of her wrist in tiny, feathery strokes.

'My pin number,' he whispered, releasing his grip. 'Keep it up your sleeve until you reach the checkout.'

Emotions churning, she pushed a loose strand of hair out of her face and raised her gaze. Focused on something normal.

'There's cat food on the list and stuff for my garden — I can't let you pay for the lot.'

He dipped his head to look into her eyes. 'You won't find it easy having us under your roof. We'll make all kinds of demands on your time and energy, however much we try not to. My paying the supermarket bill won't even come close to making up for the disruption. But it's a start.' The grin surfaced again. 'So, stop arguing and take the card.'

What could she say? To refuse would seem churlish.

'Thank you.'

His eyes burned into her as she walked towards the door. How had such a simple thing as planning a shopping trip suddenly turned so dangerous?

Ross smiled. He liked her flustered. It made an interesting change from cool, calm and collected. Maybe he should make it his mission to teach her how to have fun.

He caught himself. What about his vow to steer well clear? Any involvement with her would be setting himself up for a fall. He needed to remember that instead of wishing for things that couldn't be.

He grabbed his crutches and headed for her office. The sooner he got started on ordering the shopping, then the sooner he could shut her out of his mind.

Thankfully Ally had specified exactly what she wanted, so he only needed to tick the items on the order form. A simple enough task if Jon hadn't chosen that moment to come back downstairs and demand breakfast.

'Here . . . ' Ross handed him a pencil and a notepad he'd found by the computer. 'Sit on the carpet and draw while I finish this.'

'Bu, I want my breakfast now. And so does Pusskins.'

Pusskins? Ross glanced down to see the cat padding across the carpet.

Great. Two distractions.

'Just one minute. Then I'll get you some toast.'

Jon let the pad and pencil fall to the floor. 'Pusskins doesn't want toast, he wants . . . me to chase him.' The words ended on an excited squeal as Jon dropped on to all fours and scurried towards the cat.

'Jon, no — leave him!'

The cat shot out of Jon's reach, sending the little boy careering into the wastepaper bin.

Ross braced himself for the inevitable howls, calmed the boy down, then sent him to watch TV.

Ignoring a small, insistent voice telling him that Jon should be made to tidy the mess himself, he reached across the carpet to gather the scattered paper.

His fingers brushed something hard. What the . . . he plunged his hand deeper. A wooden photograph frame. Had Alison meant to throw this away?

He turned it over. The frame had no glass and instead of the expected photograph, a lively drawing of a cat beamed up at him. At least, he guessed it was a cat. The picture's surface was so torn and buckled that he was hard pressed to tell what the creature was. And what were these stains? Tea? Coffee? Beer? Whatever they were, the fragile paper hadn't stood much of a chance.

He ran a finger over its coarse texture. Cheap and disposable. Like the stuff wrapped around carry-outs. And judging by its brittle quality, several years old as well.

He turned the frame over. There was no clue to its age. But one thing was for sure. This picture had meant a lot to Alison. She wouldn't have bothered to frame it otherwise.

So how on earth had it got into such a state?

Realisation slammed home.

His nephews' football.

Heck.

★   ★   ★

When the boys came back from their swimming lesson, Ross took Mattie next door to collect clean clothes while Alison helped the other three children to make a sandwich lunch.

Back in his own kitchen, Ross rested against the counter, his mind still puzzling over the drawing he'd found in Alison's bin. Something had prompted him to rescue it, and like a villain from a low-budget movie, he'd tucked it into his holdall and smuggled it out of her house.

He lifted it out and stared at the mottled wood. As well as ruining the drawing, the stains had spoiled the frame's delicate primrose tint. What had once been a cheery, uplifting picture was now nothing more than a blotchy mess.

'What's that?' Mattie crossed the kitchen to peer over his shoulder.

'Just an old picture.'

'Hey, it's like the ones I used to do for Mum. I once drew her a Superman picture for her birthday and she put it in a special blue and red frame.'

That made sense. His sister-in-law had doted on her kids. But Alison was different. She didn't like children. So why had she kept this? Was the artist one of her foster brothers or sisters? A young child she'd been especially fond of? A shiver passed over him. A much-loved tot who had been adopted by another family?

He caught his breath. Was that why she didn't want children? The fear that something would happen to take them away from her?

Ross shoved the empty holdall at Mattie. 'Here, fill this with clean socks; then see if you can find my razor and my mobile phone.'

As Mattie moved away, a small seed of hope stirred in Ross's mind. If Alison had once felt strong affection for a child, then maybe that could happen again. If only he knew the full story, he might be able to hurry the moment along, persuade her to give his kids a chance?

Whoa. Not so fast. He needed to proceed cautiously here. No rushing in with a barrage of insensitive questions. He would have to await the right opportunity, then gently nudge Alison into telling him more.

Like she'd open up so easily! Accuse him of prying, more like. Whatever had put her off having kids went too deep to be solved by a simple chat.

He opened a drawer and slid the picture inside. He had to keep his suspicions under wraps. At least until he knew with more certainty that he was on the right track.

★　★　★

'Can we play out, Uncle Ross?' Mattie asked, after they'd all finished eating.

Ross looked at the boys in disbelief. Instead of their stint at the pool tiring them out, it seemed to have given them a second wind. He sighed and rubbed the back of his neck. He'd sort of promised Alison that they would watch TV, but now the thought of an afternoon cooped up in the living-room with four lively kids no longer seemed such a good idea.

'I don't see why not.'

Alison shot him a murderous look. And who could blame her, he acknowledged? She was doing him a huge favour by having them all here. So if they went in the garden, it would be on her terms. He owed her that much at least.

'There won't be any football,' he warned. 'Plus, you play in *our* garden, not Ally's. And just to make sure you don't cause any commotion, I'll be sitting on a sunlounger, watching.'

The boys gave earnest nods of agreement.

'And if Ally feels you're making too much noise,' he said, pulling his mobile phone from his pocket, 'this seems to work OK now, so she's welcome to ring and tell me. But I'm sure it won't come to that.'

Alison's face cleared. 'So what have you got planned?'

Not that planning thing again! He gave a shrug. 'I don't want to force my ideas. The kids have good imaginations. I'll sit back and see what develops.'

'Mayhem, if you're not careful.'

Was there a glint of laughter behind those silver-grey eyes?

He flashed a wide smile. 'I'm a great believer in free play. It develops the capacity for kids to think for themselves.'

Her eyebrows lifted in amusement. 'Is that right? All it seems to have developed in yours is a capacity for bickering. But we'll see.'

He shook his head. She was such a

pessimist! With him out there giving the kids his full attention, what could possibly go wrong?

★ ★ ★

Alison had only been in her office ten minutes when the trill of a telephone distracted her. It definitely wasn't hers. Had Ross left his mobile in the kitchen?

She glanced down the garden. He wasn't in sight. As a precaution against the noise, he must have taken the boys as far away from the house as possible. By the time she carried the phone over to him, the caller was bound to have rung off.

The ringing continued.

With a sigh, she followed the ring tone to the kitchen, located the phone under a tea towel, then pressed the answer button.

'Hello — Ross's phone.'

'Isn't Ross there?' asked a vaguely familiar voice.

'Not at the moment. Can I take a message?'

The voice was hesitant. 'I left a message on his answering machine yesterday, and I've been waiting to hear from him about our appointment for tonight.'

The dating agency. Alison braced herself and took a deep breath.

'I'm afraid Ross won't be able to make the meeting after all,' she said, in honeyed tones. 'Or the one tomorrow night. In fact . . . he's completely changed his mind. So it would be best if you didn't call again. Goodbye.'

She pressed the button to end the call then stared down at the phone. Why had she said that?

She had no idea.

All she knew was that it had given her immense satisfaction.

★ ★ ★

By teatime, Ross could hardly keep his eyes open. Somehow the kids had failed to grasp the idea that they were supposed to play co-operatively, and he'd spent the afternoon settling a series of disputes.

Still, these were early days. The boys had lost their parents. They were bound to be full of aggression. They just needed to understand that no amount of punching and yelling would bring back their mum and dad.

He hopped into the kitchen behind Mark and Luke, stifling a groan as they dealt each other a series of swift, surreptitious punches. Kicking their football had been a great channel of release. Maybe he could persuade Alison to let them have it back?

He had no chance to ask. After serving up their meal she took herself into her office, with a promise to be back in time for the boys' baths. He ran his hand through his hair. What on earth could he do to entertain them until then?

He had a brief respite while the boys tucked into their meal of homemade burgers. Who'd have thought Alison would take the trouble to prepare something so child-friendly? He'd half expected to find himself staring at a plate of soggy cabbage.

'Can we play out again?' Mark wiped the ketchup from his mouth and jumped down from his chair, refuelled and ready to go.

The other three followed suit.

Ross rubbed at the ache between his eyes.

'No, it's nearly bedtime.' And it couldn't come soon enough. 'Off you go into the living-room.'

'But it's still light outside.'

'The living-room! And no arguments.'

The boys scuttled.

Ross hopped to the sink and poured a glass of water. Then, setting his crutches against the draining board, he took a small plastic bottle out of his pocket and downed a couple of pre-scription painkillers. There had better be a TV programme on that the kids liked. He didn't relish another two hours spent playing referee.

Behind her closed office door, Alison smiled to herself. Somehow Ross had managed to keep the noise to a tolerable level that afternoon, but the harassed look on his face told her he'd found it a struggle.

She gave a satisfied smile. There was more than one way of bringing him round to the idea of an organised day. By this time tomorrow he would be begging her to draw up that planner.

She would put money on it.

* * *

An hour later, Alison wondered which of them would crack first. She'd ignored the first bout of squeals, confident that Ross would intervene. Instead the squeals grew louder and closer until they were right outside her office.

She gritted her teeth and yanked open the door.

The boys didn't even notice her.

They were too busy playing catch with a battered old teddy bear. A battered, bald old teddy bear with . . . a bright red ribbon around its neck.

Oh! No, no. No! They had Ben's bear.

Her furious voice jolted Ross out of his dreams.

'Why did you let them do this? You're supposed to be watching them, not letting them do exactly as they like!'

He rubbed a hand over his jaw and tried to recall what he might have done to provoke such a rush of anger. He'd played I-spy with the boys until their cartoon began, then . . . his memory blurred. The painkillers . . . combined with the white noise from the TV . . . he must have fallen asleep.

He held up his hands. 'Whatever's happened, I'm sorry, OK?'

'No, it's not OK. While you were asleep those boys of yours, they . . . '

Too overcome to finish, she slumped into a chair, tears coursing down her face.

Ross pulled himself to his feet, heart sinking to his toes. He'd failed again. Each time he thought he could cope, something happened to prove he couldn't.

'What's wrong?'

In an instant, he'd swung on to the arm of her chair. He pulled her against him, wanting to make everything all right. Soothe away her pain.

It was then that he noticed she had something clutched to her chest, her arms curled tightly around it, as if she couldn't bear to let it go.

'Tell me, Ally,' he whispered, his arms wrapped around her. 'What have the boys done to hurt you?'

'They had . . . his teddy bear.' She choked the words out on a sob. 'They were throwing it around the hall.'

His arms tightened. 'Hey, don't get upset. They often toss Jon's old saggy bear around. You'd be surprised at what that thing can withstand. It's practically invincible.'

'It isn't . . . it wasn't . . . ' She

swallowed and Ross could see she was fighting for control. 'It doesn't belong to Jon. It's the one I kept . . . after my own little boy died.'

She sagged weakly against him, as if all the life had drained out of her.

No! A cold feeling opened up inside him. He had wanted to see a chink in her armour, but not one that would cause such anguish. Not in a million years.

He buried his face in her hair. What could he say? She had lost a child and his boys had somehow got hold of this — her most precious memento.

'I'm so sorry, Ally,' he murmured, his gentle tone only serving to make the tears come faster. 'I promise they won't get away with this.'

She pulled away and palmed the tears from her eyes.

'Don't be too hard on them,' she whispered, with a catch in her voice. 'They had no way of knowing the bear was special.' She choked back a sob. 'To them it was just some old abandoned toy. I must have really scared them when I opened my door and shouted.'

'I'll be shouting, too, when I get my hands on them. Where did they go?'

'Upstairs. In fact, don't look now, but . . .'

He followed her gaze to see four woebegone faces peering through the gaps in the banisters.

'Right — ' His voice had a core of steel running through it.

'No, Ross. Please, let me.'

Slowly she stood and walked towards them.

'Come on down. No one's going to hurt you.' Her voice shook, but she stood her ground.

One by one they sidled down the stairs.

She nodded towards the sofa. 'Sit over there.'

Silence followed the order. Ross moved to sit by them, leaving Alison the vacant chair.

'Where did you find this bear?' she asked when the last boy had sat down.

'In the cupboard in the sideboard,' Mattie whispered. 'We were looking for the playing cards. Uncle Ross said he would show us how to build them into castles.'

'And when you couldn't find them, you decided to take this instead?'

Faces glum, they nodded.

Alison stroked the sparse tufts of fur on the bear's face.

'You should have asked first. This bear is really special to me, and I felt very sad when I saw you throwing it around.'

The boys exchanged troubled glances.

'We're very, very sorry, and we won't do it again,' Mattie's solemn voice assured her.

Ross shoved the last vestige of pride aside. 'I've let you down, too. I took painkillers — they knocked me out. I'm so sorry . . . I had no idea.'

Alison brushed a hand through her hair and got to her feet.

'Sorry's not good enough, I'm afraid,' she said, giving the bear one last stroke before propping it on the sideboard. 'We have to make sure nothing like this ever happens again. Stay there, all of you, until I get back.'

Without another word she marched from the room, leaving them staring after her.

'She still sounds very cross,' Mark whispered, moving closer to Ross. 'What's she going to do?'

'After what we just did, probably throw us out.'

Mattie shot him a startled glance. 'Please don't let her. I like it here. And I really, really like her.'

'So do I,' Ross murmured, struggling to suppress the twisted, hollow feeling that the thought of leaving Alison's home brought to his stomach.

'Right. Pay attention now, please, all of you.' Alison stepped back into the room, brandishing paper, felt pens, and a jumbo-sized wall calendar.

'From now we're going to have some firm rules around here, and there'll be no more do-as-you-like.' She regarded each of them in turn. 'Have you got that? This is my house and what I say goes.'

Ross found himself nodding sombrely along with the kids.

She plunked everything down on the coffee table and knelt on the carpet.

'There are a hundred and one things you can do that don't involve shouting, screaming, or rifling through my cupboards.' She picked up a pen and a sheet of paper. 'So we're going to make a list. Then we'll choose the most interesting and fill in our choices on this planner.'

A hundred and one? Ross struggled to come up with any. But after a few suggestions from Alison, ideas poured from the boys.

Twenty minutes later, she had a list nearly as long as her arm.

'Now, let's decide on tomorrow's activities. It's a choice between cooking pizza from scratch, or making paper aeroplanes. Which is it to be?'

The aeroplanes won hands-down.

'So that's what you'll be doing when you get back from the play club tomorrow,' Alison said, sending Ross a satisfied smile.

Ross grinned back, conceding defeat. He had no right to expect her to do things his way. It was bad enough that he'd taken over her life without insisting she adopt his theories. The painkillers must have affected his thinking. From now on, he would remember whose house this was and give her his full co-operation. If she wanted a clear-cut routine, then that's what she would have.

'Right, let's get that written down.' Alison flipped the pages of the planner. 'Here we are. Tomorrow is . . . Monday, the second of August.'

'The second of August?' Mattie's gaze veered toward his uncle. 'That must mean today is the first'

Ross ruffled his hair. 'Well done, Einstein.'

Mattie ducked away. 'Then . . . today is Jon's birthday.'

Ross felt a sickening lift-shaft lurch in his stomach. 'It can't be.'

'Yes, it is,' Mattie's voice was insistent. 'Mine's the first of September and Jon's is always the month before mine and now he's missed it!'

Sending A Letter To Heaven

Jon's lower lip trembled and he looked as if his world had come to an end. 'I've missed my birthday?'

'Of course you haven't.' Ross forced a note of cheeriness into his voice. 'Things have been a bit difficult this month, what with me hurting my ankle and us moving in here. So I thought we would have your birthday tomorrow.'

Mattie huffed out an exasperated breath. 'It won't be the same.'

Ross shot him a warning glance. 'Of course it will be. We'll rent a DVD and sort out some presents. There should be something in the Monday morning post from both grandmas by then, so Jon will be able to open all his presents together.'

'What about his party?' Mark piped up.

Ross tried again. 'Look, Jon's friends are all in London and he hasn't had a chance to make new ones. We'll give him a proper birthday and a proper party when we've moved back into the house next door.'

Jon gave a loud sniff.

'Jon, come on . . . '

Other than placing a comforting hand on the boy's shoulder, Ross didn't know what else to do. He might get his celebration on a different day, but he would still get one. That was the important thing, wasn't it?

The sad look in Jon's eyes told him otherwise. He had missed Jon's birthday and there was no-one else to blame. It was all his fault.

A cold knot formed in his stomach. Maybe there was something to be said for planners after all. Some things were just too important to leave to chance.

Alison wasn't sure what she had expected of Jon, but this quiet stoicism wasn't it. She felt a sudden urge to gather him close and promise that everything would be all right.

'Come on, Jon. It's time for your bath, and you can tell me what you're going to do at that special unbirthday party your uncle has planned.'

His eyes brightened. 'What's an unbirthday party?'

'You mean to say you've never had one? Then you're in for a treat. I'll tell you all about unbirthday parties while you're in the bath.'

Her eyes locked with Ross's.

'Thank you,' he mouthed, his shoulders dropping in relief.

But they both knew that the promise of a special unbirthday wouldn't pacify Jon for long.

She organised the boys' baths then saw them to bed — strictly according to age so as to avoid any disputes — and when she returned to the living-room, she could tell by Ross's absent expression that his thoughts were still on Jon.

'Don't feel too bad about the

birthday.' She tidied the paper into a pile and placed the pens on top. 'It's difficult juggling a dozen different things at once. You've had a lot going on in your life. No-one could blame you for forgetting.'

'Forgetting?' He rubbed his hands over his face. 'Until Mattie announced it, I hadn't even known when Jon's birthday was. Or any of the kids' birthdays for that matter.'

She carried the planner into the kitchen and fastened it to the wall.

'So do as you promised, then forget about it,' she called through to him, 'otherwise you'll spend the rest of your holiday trying to make things up to him.'

'That seems a bit — '

'Hard?'

She had to be hard. Otherwise the memory of the tears on the little boy's lashes would send her rushing headlong into decisions she would regret.

She walked back into the living-room. 'Ross, compassion has its negative side. If you keep it top of your list, you'll spend all holiday trying to compensate for the things that have gone wrong in the boys' lives.'

'Spoiling them, you mean?' A glimmer of laughter flashed behind his deep brown eyes. 'I know you think I'm a push-over. But this is a four-year-old we're talking about. I hate seeing him so upset.'

So did she. But there was nothing either of them could do. She bit her lip.

'I'm sorry.' She slanted a glance at Ross and her heart clenched at the expression of weary resignation on his face. 'This has been a harrowing day for us both and we need to put it behind us,' she said, sympathy softening her tone. 'I'll leave you to watch TV while I get on with my accounts. See you in the morning.'

* * *

Alison shoved away the pile of invoices. She'd been in her office half an hour and all she'd done was think of Ross.

But why? His problems weren't her problems. This wasn't the boys' home, and they had to learn that they couldn't have everything they wanted.

Except, the thing in question was a little boy's birthday and not some new-fangled toy. Every child deserved his celebrations on the right day. Being told his birthday had been postponed was like announcing that Santa wouldn't be making any deliveries this year.

She sighed and propped her chin in her hand. What if circumstances had been different and her little boy had been left without his parents? The thought of Ben's birthday going unnoticed brought a lump the size of a grapefruit to her throat.

She dashed the tears from her eyes. Ben was gone and he wasn't coming back. She should put the memories into the past and focus on her work.

But Jon was here. And desperately wishing somebody cared enough to give him a day to remember.

Her skin went cold. When had she become so selfish? So wrapped up in her own needs that she couldn't give a thought to anyone else's?

They could easily have done something to mark Jon's birthday. Sung songs, played Blind Man's Buff. Anything to make it special.

But it was too late now. The day was almost over.

Her gaze dropped to the clock on her computer screen. Too late . . . ?

There were still three hours left.

★ ★ ★

An insistent bleep ringing in his ears, Ross fought off the cloud of sleep fogging his mind. Only a smoke detector. No need to panic. His went off every time he made toast.

His eyes cut through the TV's flickering glow to the clock on the mantel.

Five minutes to midnight.

Then his brain kicked in.

Breakfast wasn't for another eight hours at least.

The sharp smell of burning filled his nostrils and he grabbed his crutches, hauled himself to his feet and swung across to the door, to find Ally on the other side of it, frantically fanning the air beneath the smoke detector with a folded newspaper.

'I'm sorry! It'll stop in a minute. There's nothing on fire.'

Dread gave way to relief. 'What happened?'

'Nothing . . . just go back into the sitting-room or else go to bed.'

Then, when he didn't move, she said, 'Ross, there's no fire . . . I can cope on my own . . . I just don't want the noise of the smoke alarm to wake the boys.'

'I'll go through to the kitchen and open the back door.'

'No!' A frantic sweep of the paper. 'I've already done it . . . everything's under control.'

He'd never seen her so flustered. Wild tendrils of hair spiralled from her ponytail, and her normally pale cheeks glowed scarlet. If the house wasn't on fire why was she so agitated?

'Maybe I'd better check anyway.' He moved towards the kitchen.

'Ross, no.' Her voice was a frustrated wail. 'If you open the door the alarm will go off again.'

But he refused to be diverted. She was hiding something. But whatever she'd done, he wasn't about to walk away and leave her to cope on her own.

He twisted the handle and pushed the door wide.

What he saw made him gasp. A mouth-watering display of open sandwiches, tiny cakes, and all sorts of other goodies, covered every available worktop. Had she done this?

He scanned the room.

The central table brought the evidence he needed. Opened bags of flour, packets of butter and empty eggshells littered the surface, while a huge stack of dirty dishes waited by the sink. Alison must have worked like a Trojan.

Why would she do this?

Then, as he looked at the cooker, he realised the cause of her panic. On the hob sat two smoking cake tins containing the charred remains of something dark and inedible.

'Ally, what's going on?'

She walked past him and poked at the contents of the cake tins.

'Isn't it obvious? I was making a cake, and now it's burned to a crisp.'

He suppressed a chuckle.

'You were baking a cake — in the middle of the night?'

'It wasn't the middle of the night when I started. I did the other stuff first then snatched a couple of minutes' rest at the table. I must have slept through the timer.' Her voice quavered. 'Now my cake's ruined and so is everything else.'

'Everything else looks fine. But what's it in aid of? I thought we'd agreed to order pizza for Jon's birthday tea?'

She turned to face him, a rueful expression on her face.

'I wanted to give Jon a late-night party. Nothing extravagant — a few games, nice food and a big squashy chocolate cake.' There was a catch in her voice. 'Just so he had something to remember.'

Ross's spirits soared. This wasn't the action of a child-hater.

'Oh, Ally.' The words came out on a groan. 'You're amazing, do you know that?'

Tears glistened on her lashes. 'If I were amazing, I wouldn't have burnt the cake.'

'Not true. You must have worn yourself out preparing this little lot. Where on earth did you get all the stuff?'

She closed her eyes and rubbed at her forehead.

'I drove to the late shopper while you were asleep. I bought balloons, cards, wrapping paper, and a big stack of fun presents, too.' Her lower lip trembled. 'But it was all for nothing. It's way past midnight and Jon's birthday is over.'

Ross's crutches thudded to the floor.

'Who says?' he murmured, his arms going round her.

'It's an indisputable fact, not a matter of opinion. The day ends at midnight. Everyone knows that.'

He leaned against the table and pulled her closer.

'I'm pretty sure Jon's too young to tell the time. I won't tell him if you don't.'

'Mattie will know.' Her words were muffled. 'And probably Mark and Luke as well. I can't see them keeping it a secret, can you?'

No, he couldn't, but he wasn't about to let a little thing like that faze him.

'Then we make another cake, get everything ready, and no matter what time we finish . . . we turn back every clock in the house to ten o'clock.'

*　*　*

There was no trouble getting Jon's brothers out of bed. The moment they heard the word 'party', they were on their feet and rushing downstairs.

207

Alison left Jon sleeping while she took the three older boys to the living room and helped them to write cards and wrap presents. Then Ross issued each little boy with a party blow-out and sent him to hide behind the sofa.

Their excitement was nothing compared to Jon's. When Ally led him into the room and his brothers jumped out yelling, 'Happy Birthday!' his face lit up with a mile-wide smile.

'It's still my birthday?' he gasped, his eyes taking in the balloons and the presents.

'It's still your birthday,' Ross assured him, nodding towards the window. 'The new day hasn't started yet. Look how dark it is outside.'

And as Jon looked, Alison snapped a switch, illuminating the darkness with dozens of flickering fairy lights.

'Ohhhh!' Jon gazed around at his family as if he couldn't quite believe it, then suddenly lunged at Alison, wrapping his arms around her waist in a fierce hug.

'Hey, your uncle helped too,' she said with a laugh. 'Who do you think untangled my Christmas lights and blew up the balloons?'

Tears glistened on her lashes.

Jon turned to his uncle, beaming fit to burst.

'Thanks, Uncle Ross. You're the best uncle in the world.'

A deep warm feeling stirred in Ross's chest. He couldn't remember the last time any of the boys had thanked him for anything. It was all he could do not to go over and hug Ally himself.

* * *

Alison had intended to start the party and then to stay firmly in the background while Ross led the boys in the games. But after two rounds of pass the parcel and hunt the slipper, she soon realised there were only a limited number of games suited to Ross's injured ankle.

So, without realising quite how it

happened, she found herself whacking balloons and racing up and down the garden with the boys, while Ross yelled encouragement from the sidelines.

The next two hours sped past in a whirl of activity ending with a traditional sit-down tea in Alison's dining-room.

She'd enjoyed herself, she realised, as she joined in with the applause when Jon blew out the candles on his cake. Despite her vow not to become involved, the family was growing on her.

For heaven's sake what was she thinking? Danger lay in that direction.

'The party's almost over,' she said, hurriedly handing round slices of cake. 'While you finish eating, I'll take the leftover food to the kitchen and then it'll be time for bed.'

A small hand clasped her arm.

She glanced down to see Jon's chocolate-smeared face gazing up at her.

'What was his name?'

She studied his thoughtful expression, unsure of what he meant.

'Your little boy,' he supplied, looking up at her with an expectant smile. 'Was chocolate cake his favourite too?'

Alison's tongue stuck to the roof of her mouth. She wanted to say that she didn't talk about Ben. That remembering hurt too much. But that would put a damper on the celebratory mood. This was Jon's special night and she wouldn't do anything to spoil it.

'His name was Ben,' she said at last. 'And he liked bacon and eggs.'

Jon gave a delighted squeal. 'My dad liked them too. He had them for breakfast every morning.'

Alison risked a glance at the little boy's face but saw only pleasure at the memory.

'Did Ben have bacon and eggs for his breakfast, like my dad?'

'Jon . . . ' Ross warned. 'Alison might not want to talk about this. Eat your cake and stop asking so many questions.'

Jon's hand slid away, and he lifted his cake to his mouth.

'No, it's all right.' Alison found herself smiling as a long-forgotten memory crept into her mind. 'I remember his very first plate of bacon and eggs. He was only two years old, and we were staying with Ben's grandma and granddad . . . and for some reason everybody got up late that morning.'

Her voice faltered as the memory unfolded. She forced herself to go on.

'When Grandma put Granddad's bacon and eggs on the table, Granddad said he hadn't time to eat them because he had to get ready for work, but we knew Granddad wanted breakfast really, so all the grown-ups rushed to help him get ready. Grandma polished his shoes, Ben's daddy went to fetch his coat and briefcase, and I made his packed lunch . . . while Granddad went off to have a shave.'

'Did Ben help too?'

Perspiration trickled down her back.

Until tonight, she couldn't even think of Ben, let alone share her memories. But some strange compulsion forced her on.

'I'm coming to that. When Granddad came back into the kitchen his breakfast was gone, and Ben was sitting at the table with egg around his mouth. 'I helped you too, Granddad,' he said. 'I ate your breakfast for you.''

Warmth filled her heart at the children's laughter. Until now she'd blotted out the memories of her son's antics, but sharing reminded her of how special he was. It felt good to remember.

'What else did he do?' The voice was Matt's. But the other boys' rapt expressions told her she had an attentive audience.

Slowly the memories resurfaced, and for the next half-hour, as she shared them, the experience was like having some small part of Ben back with her again.

'Come on, you lot,' Ross ordered

when her voice trailed off into silence. 'You've worn Ally out with all your questions. Give her a break and let her get to bed.'

'But we want — '

The mood was broken. Alison pulled herself together.

'Go and brush your teeth and then jump under the covers. First person asleep gets a big slab of birthday cake in his lunch-box tomorrow.'

That did it. They hurtled up the stairs. All except Jon. He nodded towards the bunch of helium-filled balloons that had been tied to the back of his dining chair. 'Can I have a balloon, Uncle Ross?'

Ross pretended to consider, then laughed and gently tweaked Jon's nose. 'I suppose so, seeing as it's your birthday. Which one do you want?'

Jon grabbed the string of a sunny yellow one, but instead of carrying the balloon off to bed, he held it out to Alison.

'This is for Ben.'

She fought a thickening in her throat. 'But Ben's not here, sweetie.'

Jon nodded his understanding. 'That's why you have to write him a letter.'

She took a steadying breath, looked to Ross for guidance.

'Explain to Ally what happens next,' Ross said to Jon, his voice uncharacteristically gruff.

'You fix your letter on to the string and we go out into the garden and let the balloon float up to heaven. We did that for Mummy and Daddy, didn't we, Uncle Ross?'

'That's right.' The look in Ross's eyes told Alison that he was struggling to maintain an upbeat tone. 'Only you drew a picture instead of writing a letter.'

'Can I get some paper and show Ally what to do?'

Ross sent her a searching glance, but taking the silence for assent, Jon had already run through to the living-room.

He returned a few moments later carrying the pens, paper, scissors and sticky tape that Alison had used to make the planner. Then, positioning himself at her elbow, he dropped them on to the table. 'Now, you have to think what you want to tell him.'

She hesitated. She really did *not* want to do this. But how could she refuse the little boy's request?

His brow tugged down in a frown. 'Have you thought yet?'

Alison's hand hovered over the table. She could say she was too tired. That they could do this tomorrow. But that would only delay things. The problem would still be waiting for her in the morning. She had to tackle this now.

Inhaling shakily, she picked up a pen. 'I — '

The hair at the nape of her neck prickled and for a brief, uplifting moment she felt as though a tiny ghost was there in the room with her, willing her to force the words past the lump in her throat.

'I . . . love you . . . and I miss you.'

Fingers trembling, Alison wrote down

the words and then attached the letter to the string, just below the neck of the balloon.

'And . . . ' Jon scuttled back into the living-room and returned carrying Ben's teddy bear. 'This too.'

Alison took it, not sure what to say.

'Jon, what did I tell you last time?' Ross asked with a hint of exasperation. 'A balloon won't float if you fasten on anything heavier than paper.'

Jon looked from one to the other with a small, embarrassed smile. 'Sorry, I forgot.'

'Never mind.' Ross reached for his crutches. 'You've done a great job. Let's go to the door and send Ally's balloon on its way.'

While Jon ran ahead, Ross dropped his voice to a confidential tone and said to Alison, 'Would you believe he wanted to attach a fried egg to his message to his dad?'

Her eyes misted. Poor little boy. Despite his enthusiasm he'd only half grasped the significance of releasing the balloon.

'But I won't object if you want to attach Pusskins to the end of yours,' Ross murmured, as they followed Jon through the kitchen. 'The sooner me and that cat part company the better.'

Alison suppressed the bubble of laughter rising in her throat.

'How do you do that?' she asked him, beginning to giggle.

'How do I do what?'

'Maintain such a positive outlook.'

'When the alternative is to go around feeling sad, it's not a difficult choice,' Ross whispered. 'Now, put down that teddy bear and concentrate on releasing your balloon.'

Obediently she put down the bear on the kitchen table and then went outside to join Jon on the patio.

When the thump of Ross's crutches indicated that he was there behind them, she slowly lifted her hand and released her grip on the balloon's string.

As the breeze caught the balloon and swept it into the shadowy darkness, the words of her letter repeated in her mind. '*I love you and I miss you.*'

'It's going!' Jon's voice was barely audible.

Smiling through her tears, Alison watched the balloon rise above the trees at the end of her garden. Then, a mixture of comfort and sadness churning inside, she turned away.

'Come on, Jon.' Throat aching, she squeezed out the words before her voice abandoned her altogether. 'Now it really is time for bed.'

'We can't go yet.'

'I don't see why not,' Ross said, over a yawn.

'The balloon's stuck.' Jon's voice took on a frantic tone. 'The tree's grabbed it. And won't let go.'

Alison turned to follow his gaze. He was right. The string had caught in the branches of the gnarled old apple tree.

'Uncle Ross,' Jon shrilled. 'Do something! Quick!'

'Sorry, mate, there's nothing we can do tonight. We'll have to leave it and go to bed.'

Jon stared at him with a bewildered expression. 'But Ben needs his letter.'

Alison's heart did a tiny flip-flop, and without knowing how it happened, she found herself crouching down and pulling the small boy into comforting closeness.

'The balloon will go,' she whispered. 'But maybe not straight away.'

'How?' Jon asked, in a quavering voice.

'The wind will tug it free while we're asleep.' She eased him away from her and ducked to look into his eyes. 'Come on, let's go to bed and we'll check in the morning.'

Jon pondered the matter.

'It will go, I promise.' Alison dropped a kiss on his furrowed forehead 'Thank you so much for showing me how to send my message. I feel much better now.'

'Yeah, well done, Jon.' Ross swung over and tousled his nephew's hair. 'Now, if you manage to get yourself in bed and asleep in the next five minutes, you might find your favourite biscuits in your lunchbox tomorrow.'

Jon gave a smile and raced through the open door, only to pull up short in the middle of the kitchen. 'What about the big bad wolf?'

Ross threw Alison a wry look. 'Oh, the wolf doesn't deserve biscuits.'

Jon grimaced and darted a glance towards the stairs. 'What if he followed me here and he's hiding in my room?'

Taking a deep breath, Alison picked up Ben's bear and thrust it into Jon's hands. 'Take Teddy to help you fight him off.'

Jon looked at the bear, then back at Ross as if waiting for his approval.

'If it's OK with Ally, then it's OK with me,' Ross said softly, his eyes not leaving hers.

'Of course it is.' She forced her voice to remain steady. 'This bear is a little toughie. One look at him and the wolf will run home to his den.'

With a happy smile, Jon hugged the bear to his chest, then marched towards the stairs.

'That was a huge step,' Ross whispered. 'Now let me help you take another.'

'W-what do you mean?'

Warm fingers brushed her cheek. 'Talk to me, Ally. Tell me what happened to Ben. And to your marriage.'

★ ★ ★

His heart hammered as he waited for her to answer. Why was he torturing himself by delving into her past? The loss of her child had clearly affected her marriage. Why not accept the facts instead of digging deeper? Did he really want her to spell out that she was still in love with her ex?

Yes, if it stopped him making a fool of himself. Something about the way she'd kissed him made him think he might have a chance. He had to know if he'd been deluding himself. If he'd imagined an attraction that wasn't there.

When she finally spoke her voice trembled. 'I wanted to tell you. But the memories were too painful.' She gave a half laugh. 'It was easier to let you think I didn't like children and leave it at that.'

Ross felt a rush of guilt. He should have respected her feelings. Accepted what she'd said. Instead, he'd tried to change her mind, compounding her hurt by forcing her to interact with his nephews.

'Are you sure you want to tell me?'

She gave a jerky nod. 'Tonight is the first time I've been able to talk about Ben . . . about what happened.'

'How long — ?'

'Almost four years.' She lowered her gaze and sucked in a long breath. 'Ben was practically the age Jon is now and looking forward to his fourth birthday.' Her head jerked up. 'That's what makes having you here so difficult. It brings everything rushing back.'

He laid a hand on her shoulder. 'Take your time and tell me slowly.'

'I . . . ' She stopped. Drew in a breath. 'We — '

'Go on,' he said into the silence.

'When I married I wanted lots and lots of children, and I had no reason to think I couldn't. But after I'd had Ben nothing else happened. It took over two years of shattered hopes before the doctors diagnosed endometriosis and offered an operation.'

'You went for it?'

'Oh, yes,' she whispered, with a catch in her voice. 'I was so eager, I paid for the treatment privately. Less than a month after the diagnosis I went into hospital, leaving Greg to look after Ben.'

She gazed out into the empty garden, her eyes bright with unshed tears.

'You lived here, in this house?' he asked gently.

Her chin quivered. 'Not all the time. This house needed renovating so we used it as a holiday home, tackling the repairs as and when we could afford them. We lived in a tiny flat in town at the time. There wasn't much room for Ben to play, but we managed.' Her voice faltered. 'While I was in hospital he tripped over a heap of toys and . . . '

The wobble in her voice tugged at Ross's heart. 'Injured his head?'

She closed her eyes. 'The blow knocked him out. Greg called an ambulance but it was delayed. Instead of waiting, he bundled Ben into his car and set off to drive him to the hospital himself.' She paused. 'There was a big football match on in town that day and the roads were extra busy. Greg jumped a red light and crashed the car.' Tears pooled in her eyes. 'Both he and Ben had injuries but . . . Ben's were fatal.'

'Oh, Ally.' Ross smoothed a strand of hair that had fallen across her face, wishing that he could find anything to say that could in any way comfort her.

She turned away and moved to shut the door.

'Afterwards, I couldn't face being around children. They were too strong a reminder of what I'd lost.'

Everything began to fall into place.

'But your husband thought differently?'

She secured the latch and slowly turned back to face him.

'He had always wanted a big family, and losing Ben didn't change that.' Her voice was barely above a whisper. 'Six months later he wanted to try for another baby but I couldn't bear the thought of losing another child.'

So she'd made sure that could never happen. And after her husband left she had protected herself from further hurt by refusing to get attached to anyone else?

He stared at her for a long, long minute. She was shutting him and his boys out of her life because she was scared that if she got too close to them, something might happen to snatch them away.

How could he make her see that the chances of that happening were infinitesimal? Make her realise that fear was preventing her from enjoying what could be the best years of her life?

'Ally,' he said gently, 'whenever we choose to love someone, we are opening ourselves up to being hurt. But that doesn't mean we shouldn't take the risk.'

She picked up a container of leftover sandwiches and tossed it into the fridge.

'How can you say that? After what happened to your brother, aren't you scared of something happening to one of the boys?'

He swallowed a sigh. 'That would be like giving up on life. You only get one crack at it. Why waste it worrying about things that may never happen? However difficult it seems, you have to put the past behind you and move on.'

She gave a hollow laugh. 'Like Greg did? Starting a new family and forgetting the old?'

'Can't there be room for memories of the old along with the new?'

She slammed the fridge door.

'Not if it means replacing one with

another. Greg pushing me to have another baby so soon after losing Ben was like saying Ben was expendable. That it didn't matter that Ben was no longer there.'

'And that was the reason your marriage ended?' Ross asked after a long silence. 'Because Greg was ready to move on and you weren't?'

Her anguished eyes met his. 'I didn't want Greg to go, but in the end, I had to let him. He couldn't understand that you can't replace one child with another. To him, having another child was like replacing a worn out car with a shiny new one. There was no way either of us could compromise.'

'And how do you feel about him now?' Ross asked softly.

He watched the conflicting emotions pass across her face.

'Right now, I don't know how I feel about anything.'

Of course she didn't. She'd had a tough time and needed to work through her feelings on her own. Nothing he could say would hasten the process.

Unless . . .

'One thing I learned from losing my brother is that we have to accept what we cannot control. Share our memories and feelings and then move on.' He took a deep breath. 'Sometimes it helps to find someone else who needs us.'

Wariness entered her wide, grey eyes.

'You said yourself it's been nearly four years,' he continued softly. 'Ben died but that doesn't mean you have to die too. *Time* doesn't heal. It's what you do with that time that matters.' He reached for her hand and curved his fingers around hers. 'You need to move out of safe boundaries and make new friends and new opportunities.'

He ached to wrap his arms around her. Kiss those trembling lips. But the faint smile she cast him was so sad and vulnerable that he couldn't bring himself to put any more pressure on her.

'The boys could help you,' he said instead. 'If only you'd let them into your life.' His thumb whisked over her knuckles in a soothing gesture. 'Not as a replacement for the child you lost, or the ones you never had. But for who they are and the fun they could bring.'

She looked at him for a long moment, then with a regretful smile she pulled her hand from his grasp.

'If you don't mind, it's been a long day . . . '

'Of course. I'm sorry.'

A twist of regret gripped his stomach. Maybe the word fun had been a bad choice. He'd only been trying to make her see that there was no disloyalty in living and loving again. That fun and laughter could help her re-enter life.

'Ally — ' he began, in an awkward voice.

Without looking at him, she moved off towards the hall. 'Goodnight, Ross.'

He slashed a hand through his hair, feeling helpless.

Alison ran upstairs to her room and flung herself on her bed. What an idiot! For a moment there, when Ross had urged her to find someone else who needed her, she'd thought he was about to tell her that he was that someone. And her foolish heart had soared at the prospect. What in the world had got into her? How could she even think of involving herself with a man like Ross?

Not withstanding that his interest in her came more from pressing child care needs than genuine affection, his reckless approach to life made him the worst possible man for her.

But that knowledge didn't stop her from feeling things about him that she'd never felt for any man before. Making her want things she'd thought impossible.

Alison bit her lip. Writing that message to Ben had helped her to get her emotions in order. Maybe setting her thoughts down on paper could help again. Make her realise that this sudden lapse in common sense was nothing more than an over-the-top reaction to Ross's flair for lifting her mood.

With a sweep of her fingers Alison

pulled Claire Samuels' notebook from under the bed, then switched on her bedside light.

If she analysed her feelings clearly and precisely, she would soon be over these silly yearnings.

Alison Takes A Risk

For the first time in years, Alison slept until late morning. Ross was already up and dressed when she came downstairs, and she sheepishly accepted his offer of a mug of steaming coffee. He'd done nothing to warrant her sharp reaction last night. She shouldn't have taken her frustrations out on him.

'I'd better ring the play scheme organiser and apologise for the boys' late appearance,' she said, the faint tremor in her fingers contradicting her calm voice. 'Do you think a spontaneous midnight party is an acceptable excuse?'

He darted her a sideways glance. 'She accepted it when I put it to her earlier.'

'You've spoken to her already?'

He sipped his coffee and studied her over the rim of his cup, a teasing glint in his eyes. 'Some of us have been awake since eight o'clock. Now, would you like birthday cake or sandwiches with your coffee? I thought we'd skip breakfast and eat the party leftovers for brunch. That way the boys don't miss out on the promised cake.'

At the mention of the word 'cake', footsteps clattered on the stairs, and Matt appeared in the doorway.

'Cake for breakfast? Yum!' His eyes sparkled.

'You have to earn it, I'm afraid.' Ross opened the fridge and lifted out a container of sandwiches and the remainder of Jon's chocolate birthday cake. 'Dash upstairs and tell your brothers to get dressed. We want to get going in the next hour.'

'You're . . . ?' Alison fought off a wave of disappointment. 'I must have misunderstood. I thought I was taking the boys to the play scheme today.'

He looked at her with a curious expression. 'I need to find Jon a present so I've organised a taxi to take me into town. I'll drop the boys off on the way.'

Alison sipped her coffee. She couldn't argue with his logic. So why did some irrational part of her wish that she was going with them?

For a while it looked as though Ross might meet his one-hour deadline. Mark and Luke dressed in record time and ate their food without questions. But when Jon came downstairs he refused breakfast and headed straight to the window.

'Oh, no! Look! Ben's balloon is still stuck, Uncle Ross,' he said.

'What balloon?' Matt knelt on his chair and strained to see.

'It's a messenger balloon for Ally's little boy.' Jon turned to face his brothers with a woebegone expression. 'She sent it last night but it's stuck in the tree. I need Uncle Ross to make it go.'

'I'll climb up and get it,' Luke shouted, climbing out of his chair.

'No, you won't! I'm much better at tree climbing.' Mark grabbed his brother's T-shirt and attempted to haul him back.

'I'm the eldest — it should be me.' Mattie sent his uncle a pleading look.

Ross drained his coffee cup. 'OK. Outside, everyone, let's get this sorted.'

With a whoop, the boys charged into the garden.

Alison stopped with her coffee cup halfway to her mouth. 'Ross — what are you planning to do?'

'Isn't it obvious? We're going to free the balloon.'

'We?' She gave his crutches a pointed look.

He grabbed the crutches and hauled himself to his feet. 'OK, Mattie is. But he needs us to cheer him on.'

He ignored her small cry of protest and hobbled to the garden.

'Ross, you can't. It's far too danger-ous. What if he were to fall?'

'He won't.'

'You can't know that. I won't let you do it.'

She cupped her hands around her mouth. 'Luke! Mark! All of you. The taxi's on its way. Grab your football and wait by the front gate.'

'What about the balloon?' Matt's voice was indignant.

'It'll still be there when you get back.' She kept her tone firm. 'Come on, quick, quick! First person to the gate gets to sit in the front seat.'

As the boys raced past her, Ross shook his head. 'Alison, there's no need for this. You're exaggerating the risk out of all proportion.'

'But you admit there *is* a risk?'

He looked straight at her. 'Of course there is. And I wouldn't want it any other way.'

'I can't believe you just said that. Haven't you any sense of danger?'

'Alison, you're being irrational. Facing risks builds confidence. Forces people to develop gutsy attitudes. You should try it sometime.'

'This isn't about me,' she yelled, the words bursting from her throat. 'It's about you allowing Matt to climb that tree. Children need to be kept safe, and it's your responsibility to see that that happens.'

He shook his head and met her outraged gaze with a look of exasperation.

'No, you're wrong. It's constantly seeking safety that's dangerous. It might bring comfort in the short term but ultimately it makes people less safe.'

'How?'

He watched her closely. 'By reducing their ability to handle stress.'

Alison ran her hands through her hair. 'So you're saying that you can inoculate the boys against stress by exposing them to danger?'

'Not danger — but well-chosen challenges, which I know they can face with success.'

'Danger . . . challenges. What's the difference? Rationalisation won't make what you're doing any less risky. You have four energetic boys who tend to think before they act. You should be monitoring them carefully — not encouraging reckless bravado.'

'Don't mistake what I'm doing for

recklessness. There's a world of difference between the kind of risks I'm suggesting and your husband impulsively jumping a red light.'

'Not from where I'm standing.'

Ross gazed at her for a long moment. 'It's all to do with acting calmly. My decisions might be quick but they're not foolhardy. I'm training the boys to approach their challenges with level heads. To stay in control and fight their panic.' A hint of wistfulness entered his words. 'That same attitude could help you abandon your rut if only you'd let it.

'Think about it, Alison.' His jaw was tense. 'Do you really want to end up a lonely, workaholic singleton? Because that's exactly where you're headed.'

With that, he followed the boys up the path, leaving her staring after him.

★   ★   ★

Half an hour later, Ross's hurtful phrase still ringing in her ears, Alison plunged a heavy metal spade into the dry earth of a flower bed. His words had left her so agitated that she hadn't been able to settle to her work, opting for a vigorous gardening session instead.

She ripped out a clump of weeds and hurled it into her wheelbarrow. She knew what Ross was doing. Projecting his inadequacies on to her, because he was too stubborn to admit that he was risking Mattie's life for something as trivial as a balloon.

She dropped her spade and turned to look again at the tree. It was far too high for a boy of Mattie's size. She had been right to stop him from going up there. This was her garden, and she called the shots. The balloon could stay where it was.

So what about Jon?

She gave a mental shrug. The balloon would either burst or shrivel to nothing and Jon would assume the wind had carried it off.

She strode across the grass to take a closer look. Hmmm. Maybe the solution wasn't quite as straightforward as she'd thought. The balloon might soon disappear but the letter would survive longer. The sight of it gradually disintegrating could destroy the comfort Jon had gained from the ritual and make him wonder whether his own message to his parents had met a similar end.

She either had to trust Ross's judgement and allow Matt to go up and release it, or let Jon suffer emotional distress.

Unless . . . Alison fingered the tree's trunk. There was nothing to stop her from climbing up there, was there?

For a long time she stood gazing up into the branches. She wanted to walk away, but some inner compulsion forced her to grab the lowest branch and haul herself up the trunk. Her stomach churning, she looked around. There were plenty of footholds; the bark was dry. If she really put her mind to it, she could make it to the top. If only she could push through the fear.

What had Ross said? Stay in control.

Fight the panic. Maybe if she took strength from Ross's attitude and looked on this as an adventure rather than a problem, the panic would go away.

With her heart pummelling her ribs, she focused her gaze on the balloon, and in a series of slow steady movements hauled herself towards her target. Twigs gouged her arms and leaves blocked her vision but she forced herself onwards and upwards, Ross's words replaying in her head.

Then she was there, at the top of the tree, inches away from the balloon.

Breathing heavily, her back wet with sweat, she hooked one arm over a branch and used the other to free the string.

The balloon soared into the open sky until it was nothing more than a tiny yellow speck.

'Love you, Ben,' she whispered.

★ ★ ★

Ross stared around the toy store. Every imaginable plaything filled the shelves: go-karts, punch balls, water pistols. How on earth was he supposed to make a decision? If only he had Alison with him. She'd know exactly what to choose.

Maybe he should phone her. His hand went to his pocket and then fell away. After what he'd said, he'd be lucky if she ever spoke to him again, never mind help him out of a pickle.

He leaned on his crutches, trying to quell the image of those wounded grey eyes.

Last night, she'd trusted him enough to share her memories. But instead of building on that, and gradually encouraging her to move out of her safe boundaries, he'd tried to force the pace.

'Do you need any help?' The saleswoman's voice snapped him back to the present.

He smiled at her as she came out from behind the counter.

'I'm looking for a birthday present

for a four-year-old.'

She eyed his plaster cast and gave him an answering smile.

'You're obviously not in any fit state to zoom around the displays. I'll find you a seat and then I'll show you our catalogue.'

He gave a grateful nod, and waited while she brought a stool from the office.

'We have climbing frames, trampolines, trapeze bars . . . ' the saleswoman recited, as he eased himself into a comfortable position on the stool. She flipped through the pages of the catalogue, then paused to hold up an illustration of a selection of outdoor toys.

Ross felt a rush of enthusiasm. Any of them would be a great way to encourage Jon's sense of adventure, and the other kids could join in the action too. They would have a good time.

'Or, if you'd prefer quieter, more creative activities,' the woman added, 'we have build-your-own wooden pirate ships and castles, art materials, board games, construction sets . . . ' She flipped the pages of the catalogue again and pointed to a picture of happy, absorbed children all busy creating.

Hmm . . . What should he opt for? Had Alison been with him, she'd have urged him to choose quiet and controlled over rowdy and daredevil. But would the kids go for it?

He squared his shoulders. He shouldn't be thinking like this. They'd go for whatever he bought them, providing that he showed the necessary enthusiasm; Alison's impromptu party had surely taught him that. If he wanted her to trust his judgement, then he should start trusting hers.

She'd suggested calmer activities for the boys, and he'd accused her of wanting to feminise them. She'd wanted rules and routines and he'd scoffed. Why? Because he believed boundaries were incompatible with an adventurous lifestyle? Or was he using that as an excuse to take an easier path?

His stomach tightened. Maybe Alison wasn't the only one who needed to face hard truths. Was he so unsure of how to control the kids' behaviour that he barely tried?

He gazed at the page of tabletop activities.

'Do any of these help develop social skills?'

'It says here that with adult super-vision, they help develop concentration, turn-taking, sharing, following simple rules and instructions . . . '

Ross gave an answering smile and reached for his wallet.

'That's good enough for me. I'll take a build-your-own pirate ship, a box of art materials, a compendium of board games and . . . anything else that might keep four little hoodlums quiet.'

★ ★ ★

After finding her way back down the tree, Alison repeated the climb, then swung off a low branch to land with a thud at the base of the trunk, almost dizzy with exhilaration. Nothing bad had happened. She'd taken a risk and come out of it all in one piece.

Excitement bubbled inside her. So why stop there? Why not shin up the small oak tree in Ross's cousin's garden, too? Push herself to her limits.

And what if Ross came back and caught her? The thought made her squirm. It was one thing to admit to herself that she'd been wrong and he'd been right. It was quite another to admit it to him. Right or not, his words had been insensitive and thoughtless, and she wasn't ready to let him off the hook just yet.

Still on a giddy high, she skipped across the lawn and back to her office. Maybe her climb was a sign. Some risks were worth taking. Some risks were fun!

★ ★ ★

She needn't have worried about Ross catching sight of her up the tree. He didn't get back until mid-afternoon, and after popping his head round her office door to let her know that one of the other parents would see the boys home, he headed straight round to his cousin's house next door.

Good. Alison rearranged a stack of files on her desk, slamming one on top of the other. He probably realised he'd overstepped the mark this morning, and knew when to make himself scarce.

She pushed the files to the back of her desk and sat down in her chair. With Ross out of the way she'd be able to get on with her work without interruption. But what should have been relief felt more like disappointment. Ridiculous. Climbing that tree must have softened her brain.

Ross timed his return to Alison's house to coincide with the boys' arrival home from the play scheme, and Jon's happy shouts told her that Ross had chosen his birthday present wisely. She wondered what it was. She only hoped that morning's post had brought presents from the grandparents too.

Alison didn't have to wait long to find out. The noise had scarcely settled when Jon burst into her office.

'Ally, Ben's balloon's gone!'

As she looked down at his beaming, upturned face, a warm rush of affection overwhelmed her.

'Hey, that's great.'

He grabbed her hand. 'Will you come and see my birthday presents?'

She bent down and swept the little boy into a spontaneous hug. 'Of course I will. Lead the way.'

Jon led her into the living-room, where Ross was perched on a chair arm, supervising some kind of colouring activity on the coffee table.

He gave a rueful glance. 'Sorry to drag you from your work, but Jon couldn't wait to tell you about the balloon.'

'I wish I could have climbed up to it.' Matt's sigh was wistful. 'Uncle Ross says I'm not allowed up there now the balloon's gone.'

Alison crouched to bring herself down to his level.

'Maybe we'll have a tree-climbing afternoon soon. The apples are almost ready for picking. We'll have a competition to see who can collect the most.'

Surprise lit Matt's eyes. 'Really? We can go up your tree?'

'Uh-huh.' Alison sent Ross an if-it's-OK-with-you look. 'So long as you wear the right kind of shoes and go carefully, I can't see a problem. In fact, I might even join you.'

Ross gave a snort of disbelief.

Alison straightened and gave him her sweetest smile. 'So, where are these presents?'

Jon ran to the sideboard.

'Uncle Ross got me a special pirate ship. One I have to build myself. Then there's a box of paints, some crayons, and lots of other stuff to share. Oh, and Grandma Claire sent me some DVDs.'

'She sent presents for the rest of us, too.' Matt pointed to a small stack of computer games under the table.

'Uncle Ross says we can take it in turns to go next door with him to play them. But right now we have to do our thankyou pictures.'

Thank-you pictures? Alison's gaze went to a huge collection of felt tipped pens in the centre of the table.

'Are the pens from Jon's other grandparents?' she wondered.

'No, their present still hasn't arrived.' Ross looked at her silently for a moment as if he was unsure what to say next. 'The pens are from me.'

'You?' It was her turn to look surprised.

He gave a shrug. 'You wanted us to do something more tranquil, so I invested in a set of art materials. The kids are making thank-you cards for their Grandma Claire.'

Luke propped his chin in his hands and gave a regretful sigh. 'I miss Grandma Claire. Why doesn't she come to see us any more?'

Ross folded his arms across his chest. 'Because we're on holiday.'

'She could still come though, couldn't she?' Luke persisted.

Mark looked up. 'Doesn't she like us any more?'

'Of course she likes you.' Ross swiped a hand through his hair. 'But grandmas don't usually follow their grandkids on holiday. Although,' he added, through clenched teeth, 'I wouldn't put it past this one.'

'I want her to come, too.' Jon's chin wobbled. 'I want to tell her about my party.'

Ross's face took on a weary look. 'Tell her in your picture. If you draw that big squashy chocolate cake and everyone playing games, she'll know what a good time you had.'

Alison studied the dejected set of the boys' shoulders. Couldn't Ross see what his feud with their grandmother was doing to them?

'A phone call would be more personal,' she said, with deliberate casualness. 'And it would give the boys the reassurance they need.'

Ross sucked in a breath through his teeth.

'That'd mean I'd have to speak to her,' he murmured in a voice only Alison could hear. 'Which is something I'd rather not do.'

'Ross, the boys need their grandmother in their lives.' The words were out before she could stop herself. She cleared her throat and continued in a quieter voice. 'If only the two of you could co-operate instead of fighting.'

'Small chance of that,' he continued in the same low murmur. 'She doesn't understand the meaning of the word.'

Alison looked him straight in the eye. 'Do you mean to tell me you can't even speak to each other on the phone without falling out?'

Matt looked up. 'When Grandma Claire rings Uncle Ross, he gets cross and shouts a lot,' he confided with an impish grin.

Ross ruffled the boy's hair.

'Can you wonder? I swear that woman was trained by the Spanish Inquisition.'

Alison jerked her head in the direction of the open door and waited for Ross to follow her out of the room.

'She lost her daughter — maybe she worries.' She felt compelled to fight the boys' grandmother's corner. 'What you see as interference could just be a bad case of anxiety.' She looked at him closely. 'Heaven knows I'm guilty of it myself.'

His eyes momentarily darkened. 'The woman hates me. It's as simple as that.'

'If you could make her see that her grandchildren are well and happy, she would probably change her mind.' Just as she had.

Where had that thought come from? This morning she'd accused the man of being reckless and irresponsible. Surely Ross hadn't changed since then.

No. She was the one who had changed. Loath as she was to admit it, this morning's clash had led to a new understanding. Ross wasn't some clue-less risk taker, but an intelligent and caring guardian, struggling through his inexperience to build the boys' self-confidence and self-reliance. He needed support, not condemnation.

And if she could see that, maybe Claire Samuels would eventually come to realise it too.

Ross gave a deep sigh. 'And how do I do that when she doesn't believe anything I tell her? The instant she hears my voice, she's ready to criticise.'

'Then let Mattie make the call,' she said. 'He's old enough to do it sensibly. He can put his brothers on one at a time while you stay on the sidelines. The responsibility will do him good. He'll be falling over himself to prove how grown up he is.'

'Can I, Uncle Ross?'

They turned to see that the boys had followed them out into the hall.

'We'll be really sensible,' Mark joined in, 'won't we, Luke?'

Luke gave a vigorous nod.

Ross breathed deeply before he answered. 'I'm not sure it's a good idea.

Once you start telling your grand-mother all your news she'll find out I've hurt my ankle, and . . . ' his voice trailed off.

Mattie gave a wide grin. 'I could leave that bit out.'

Slowly Ross's tense frown relaxed into a smile.

'OK, you've got me.' He pulled his mobile phone from his pocket and scrolled through the directory. 'Right, here's her number, Mattie. Grab some paper and write it down.'

With the air of one entrusted with enormous responsibility, Matt wrote down the number as Ross read it out, then carried the note over to the phone and keyed it in. His quick thumbs-up indicated he'd managed to get through.

'Hey, Grandma, guess who . . . No, everything's fine . . . Uncle Ross thinks I'm old enough to ring by myself now . . . Thank you for . . . Oh . . . ' His expression switched to disappointment. 'All right, then . . . Bye.'

Alison's heart sank. Such a brief call

was worse than none at all.

'What did she say?'

Matt dropped the slip of paper by the phone and gave a nonchalant shrug. 'To ring later. She's . . . '

'Too busy polishing her cauldron?' Ross muttered to Alison.

Matt gave him a blank look. 'She's off to the hairdresser's and can't talk now.'

'That's rich,' Ross whispered, as Matt went to join his brothers. 'She accuses me of not being sensitive to their needs, then knocks them back for a hairdressing appointment.'

Alison suppressed a sigh. The distressed woman who'd turned up on her doorstep cared too much about her grandchildren to treat them in such a cavalier fashion. Why couldn't Ross see that?

'Have some sympathy. London hairdressing appointments are booked months in advance. You can't expect her to miss out because of a phone call she didn't expect.'

She turned to face the boys. 'Did your grandma say when she would be able to talk, Matt?'

His brow puckered. 'When she gets back from the hairdresser's she's got to get ready to go out.' His face suddenly cleared. 'But she's at home tomorrow and the day after that and she wants me to phone again so we can have a lovely long chat.'

'I know her lovely long chats,' Ross murmured, turning away so the boys wouldn't hear. 'Interrogation might be a more fitting description.'

'But you'll give her the benefit of the doubt and let Matt try again?'

He tipped his head on one side. 'Why are you so keen to take her part?'

Alison's heart missed a beat. Did he suspect that she and Claire had met? Maybe he'd seen Claire's car that day she'd called round. No. If that were the case he'd have said something before now. 'I — '

His gaze rested speculatively on her face.

'There are no sides in this, Ross. It's easy to see you both want what's best for the boys. The sad thing is you have such opposing ideas of what that means.'

He looked a little surprised at the seriousness of her tone. Alison swallowed hard. She should shut up now. She would only cause increased curiosity if she continued to fight Claire's cause.

'Don't stop there,' he said with an edge to his voice. 'If you've something to say then spit it out.'

'OK. You're convinced you're doing fine on your own, and she probably feels you're floundering and that her advice is essential. I know she's trying your patience. But whatever your feelings for the woman, anyone can see the boys want her around. So, for their sakes, why not leave her number here and let them ring two or three times a week? It might help build a few bridges and get the two of you on friendlier terms.'

She propped Matt's slip of paper by the phone.

'Hey, I agreed to one phone call. I'm not out to make her my new best friend.'

'If you don't want her zooming up the motorway to check up on you, then one phone call isn't enough, not by a long chalk. What does it matter if she finds out about your broken ankle? The boys are well looked after here. Between us we're doing a pretty good job.'

His eyes sparkled. 'We do make a good team, don't we?'

She kept her gaze neutral.

'OK, you win,' he said. 'The boys can phone her. I just hope I don't regret this.'

Alison let out a long sigh. The person most likely to regret it was her. When Claire Samuels realised the family was living under her roof, she'd expect a thorough report.

What had she got herself into?

A Surprise Proposal

After they'd all eaten, Alison continued with her work until the boys' bedtime. She supervised their baths, then sent each boy in turn downstairs to sit with Ross.

'Right, bed in five minutes,' she announced, as she followed Matt into the living room. 'Then your uncle can watch TV in peace. In fact,' she added, shooting a tentative smile in Ross's direction, 'I might even join him. It's been ages since I've spent an evening in front of the television.'

Ross looked up and gave an awkward smile. 'Sorry, but I won't be here. I'm taking Matt next door to try out those new computer games.'

Mark and Luke gave a collective groan.

'And before you say it's not fair . . . ' Ross continued in a firm tone ' . . . your turn will come. I'll be taking someone different each night.'

Alison's heart sank to her toes. Was Ross deliberately avoiding spending time with her?

The next day, he couldn't even wait until the evening before returning to his own house. Alison came home from dropping the boys at the play scheme, to find he'd left her a note.

'Ally, gone next door again. Need to send a few e-mails and arrange for a cleaning agency to sort out the house ready for when we move back in.'

She settled in front of her computer with a sigh. So, he was already thinking about leaving. How ironic. When she'd finally let go of Ben and felt ready to build a future, Ross's interest in her had waned.

She pushed away from her desk and walked over to the window. If she wanted proof that Ross had only wanted her for her childcare skills, then maybe this latest incident was it. Sunday night's revelations had changed things. Now that he thought her emotional problems too deep to overcome, the flirting had ceased.

She pressed her forehead against the cool glass. Oh, why couldn't she have kept her emotions under wraps? It didn't take a genius to figure out he'd headed off next door because he needed a bolthole. She should put him out of her mind and concentrate on her work.

But how could she? The excitement she'd felt for her work had evaporated, leaving a strange feeling of restlessness in its place. All she could think of was how big the house felt with no boys and no Ross. Was this what her life would be like once the family had gone? Dull. Boring. Empty.

A shiver ran through her, and despite the heat of the day she felt bleak and cold. Did she really want to spend the rest of her life on her own — loving no-one and no-one loving her?

She lifted her head and stared through the window at the empty garden.

The man who could change that

vision of emptiness was only yards away. Maybe she should go over there now. Take a leap into the unknown and tell him how she felt?

Hey, slow down a minute! What had happened to the woman who kept a lid on her emotions? The woman who'd pushed Ross to build a tall fence between her house and his?

Alison closed her eyes and replayed the fantasy image of four little boys playing at the water's edge, while she and Ross looked on. The image tore at her heart. Was the reality really so far out of reach? Supposing she told Ross that she yearned to have children in her life again?

The temptation was strong, but no matter how enticing the vision, her part in it had to be more than a convenience. Could she really build a life with Ross knowing that she wasn't wanted for herself; that he only wanted her as a childminder?

The answer came back as a resounding 'no'. She wanted a warm, passionate relationship with everlasting love. But she wanted it with Ross.

Her heart pounded. She had no idea how it had happened, but she'd fallen in love with the man. That heightened awareness whenever their gazes meshed, her insides turning to jelly at his slightest touch, and that fidgety, unsettled feeling whenever he was gone — all pointed to the same conclusion. She loved him and she wanted him.

When the feeling had first surfaced she didn't know. Maybe it was the moment she'd seen him on the hospital trolley, overcome with pain but somehow managing to reassure the boys and make them laugh. Or maybe it had been even earlier — the morning he'd chased her around the kitchen. All she knew was that instead of acting on the attraction, she'd been so afraid of once again being left crushed and alone that she'd denied the feeling and pushed him away.

If only she hadn't. If only she'd been

brave enough to take a risk. Now, thanks to her stupid caution, her love wasn't returned.

So deal with it!

How? She'd given him no reason to love her. She might as well have had the words KEEP OFF tattooed across her forehead for all the encouragement she'd offered. And no matter how much she wished things could be different it was too late to change things now.

Are you sure about that?

For a long moment Alison didn't move, then she pushed back her shoulders and walked towards the door. The old Alison might sit and mope, but the new one was different. She climbed trees, took risks, made things happen.

A short while later, she strode across the lawn to the house next door, carrying a slice of birthday cake and a mug of coffee. She would start small — take Ross a mid-morning snack, and gradually work up to cooking him a romantic dinner.

But when she reached Ross's back

door, it was slightly ajar. Through the gap she spotted him leaning against the kitchen counter, a phone propped between his chin and shoulder. She paused to balance the mug on the plate and lifted her hand to knock, but Ross's voice halted her in her tracks.

'See you soon, Maria. The boys would be turning cartwheels if they knew I'd rung you. I've told them what great fun you are.' He gave a warm laugh. 'No, I'm not telling them we're going on a date.' Another laugh. 'All in good time. I need to pick the right moment.'

Alison felt as though her insides were being ripped apart. What was she doing here? Ross wasn't interested in building a relationship with her. He'd already crossed her off his list and moved to the next in line. Goodbye, Alison — hello, Maria.

Gripping the mug so tightly that her fingernails dug into her palm, she hurried back to her kitchen, the green-eyed monster roaring inside her head.

She'd just saved herself major embarrassment. From now on she would keep
her feelings firmly under wraps. Restraint
was the only solution.

★ ★ ★

Ross didn't return to Alison's house
until the boys were due home. Then
he surprised her by announcing that he
wanted her to have a night off from
cooking and that he'd order a takeaway
later for the boys' supper..

Alison prepared a light sandwich
snack for him and the boys, then she
left them playing board games while
she took her sandwiches into her office
for her usual late afternoon stint of
working on her clients' accounts.

When she returned to the living-
room a couple of hours later, it was to
find the boys curled up in front of the
TV and Ross looking more dressed-up
than Alison had ever seen him.

'Going somewhere?'

He gave her an easy smile. 'I hope so.'

'I see.'

Her gaze travelled over the curling shower-damp hair, past the crisp dark blue shirt and down to a pair of smart black chinos. He must have painstakingly unpicked the end of one of the seams as the trouser leg neatly accommodated his plaster cast. She only hoped Maria appreciated the trouble he'd gone to.

'Why won't you tell us where you're going, Uncle Ross?'

Before Ross could answer, the doorbell rang.

He raised an eyebrow. 'Alison, would you mind . . . ?'

'Of course not,' she said, trying to sound as normal as possible, but the leaden lump in her chest made her voice come out a little strained.

Maria stood on the doorstep, looking gorgeous in a turquoise halter-necked dress that showed off her beautiful olive skin.

'Hi, Alison,' she said, in a breathy voice. 'I'm not too early, am I? Ross said eight o'clock, but I couldn't wait.'

A wave of jealousy, so powerful it made her gasp, ricocheted through Alison's body. 'I — he — '

Maria's brow furrowed. 'He hasn't told you, has he?'

Alison shook her head.

'No, but I'm about to,' came Ross's voice from behind her. 'Ally, Maria is here to baby-sit. I've arranged to take you for a special thank-you dinner.'

Heart skittering, Alison's mind raced. She shouldn't attach any special significance to the gesture. It was probably nothing more than a tactful way of getting her out of the house while Maria got to know the boys.

'Why didn't you tell me?'

'I thought you might say no.'

'I can still say no.'

His mouth kicked up in a lopsided smile. 'But now you have to say it to Maria as well, and that makes it a lot harder to refuse.'

Harder, but not impossible.

'I'm afraid I'm going to anyway.' She

let out a shaky breath. 'I've had a headache brewing all day, and I really need to lie down.' She hoped she sounded convincing.

Maria glanced sideways at Ross. 'The best cure for a headache is a relaxing night out. Isn't that right, Doctor?'

Doctor? Alison had assumed that Ross was unemployed — that he was one of those people who picked up jobs as and when he needed to earn money.

Maria must have seen her stunned expression. 'Oh, don't say he didn't tell you that, either.'

Ross gave a shrug. 'Sorry. I didn't think it was important.'

Maria rolled her eyes. 'Can you fathom it? He's a gifted surgeon and he doesn't even think it worth mentioning.'

'So, to get back to your original question, Maria — ' Ross adopted a mock admonishing tone. 'I agree. The patient's headache should go once she's in a stress-free environment.'

He turned to smile at Alison.

'So take two paracetamol and come out with me. We're not going far. You can easily come home if things don't improve.'

Maria clasped her hands in front of her chest in a pleading gesture

'Come on, Alison, you can't disappoint me. I'm really looking forward to baby-sitting, and so is Ned.'

'Ned?'

'My husband.' Maria glanced up the street. 'He'll be here in a minute. He's just parking the car.' She turned back to face Alison and gave a little jiggle of impatience. 'Oh, I can't wait any longer — I just have to tell you. We're having a baby. We hit the crucial three months tomorrow, so I reckon it's all right to tell you now.'

The knot of unease in Alison's chest began to ease.

'That's fantastic. You must be so excited.'

'We are.' Maria turned again as a tall, broad-shouldered man appeared at the gate. 'But would you believe that Ned's starting to panic? He hasn't a clue about kids, so when Ross asked me to baby-sit, Ned begged to come too. I hope you don't mind?'

'I suppose that means you'll want the boys to stay up and play?'

Ned jogged up the path in time to catch the tail-end of Ross's words.

'That'd be great if they could.' His voice matched his physique — rugged and tough. A typical man's man. Probably the youngest in a family of boys, and no idea which end of a baby the nappy went on.

Maria sent Alison another pleading look. 'You can't disappoint us now. Not when my poor husband has been so looking forward to it.'

Ross's dark eyes glinted mischievously. 'Come on, Alison. How can you refuse a request like that?'

Her heartbeat quickened. This could turn out to be nothing more than a thank-you dinner, or signal the start of a deep and lasting relationship. She had no way of knowing. But if she didn't go, she would never find out.

'OK,' she said, her heart tripping and skipping in her chest. 'You organise the takeaways for the boys' supper while I dash upstairs and change.'

Ross released the breath he'd been holding. For a moment he'd feared an unplanned night out would be too much for Ally, but apart from one small token protest she hadn't really objected. Was this a sign she was opening up her mind to new possibilities? Possibilities that included a future with him? Hey, one step at a time, remember? Move too fast and you'll scare her away.

His resolve weakened fifteen minutes later when Alison came downstairs. By then he'd introduced Maria and Ned to the boys and they were in the living-room playing a rowdy game of tiddlywinks while Ross waited in the hall.

Alison's dress changed her entirely. He'd only ever seen her in black or white, her hair tied back in some sort of tightly-restrained arrangement.

'I hope this is dressy enough.'

She looked down at her vivid pink and gold slip dress then back up at him, her lips curving into a smile.

He ached to tell her that she looked earth-shatteringly beautiful, to kiss that tempting mouth. But doing that would give away his feelings and she wasn't ready for that.

'You haven't said where we're going,' she reminded him.

'It's a surprise.'

'But I'll do?'

'You'll more than do — you look perfect.'

A strange feeling of tightness attacked his chest and brought the urge to clear his throat.

Self-consciously she pushed an escaped tendril of hair away from her face to join the pale ripple of waves tumbling down her back.

She was watching him almost as carefully as he watched her. Was she feeling the same distraction? Experiencing the same desire? He had no way of knowing. All he knew was, she needed time to explore whatever feelings she had for him and the boys. Time to come to terms with those feelings and let them grow. And unless he kept scrupulously to his resolution to take things slowly, those feelings would never develop.

He tightened his grip on his crutches and deliberately turned away. 'I think I just heard our taxi.'

★   ★   ★

'A surprise?' Alison settled into the taxi with scarcely concealed excitement. 'I hope this isn't another attempt to stir up my spontaneity. Please tell me I won't find myself eating raw fish or singing karaoke.'

Was she more relaxed than usual? It was hard to tell. There was something different about her and it wasn't just the clothes. She sounded lighter, more playful.

'I promise there'll be nothing embarrassing,' he whispered, twisting to face her. 'But to get full benefit you have to close your eyes.' As he spoke, he slipped an arm around her slender shoulders and covered her eyes with both his hands. 'So, come on, now. No peeping until I give the word.'

Momentarily she stiffened, then her shoulders dropped and she relaxed against him with a light laugh. But he didn't miss the flush on her cheeks or the way her breathing quickened as if her lungs were suddenly short of air. Physically she was attracted to him, he was sure. But mentally, was she ready for a new relationship? Would she eventually come to feel the same way that he did? Only time would tell.

The journey was over all too quickly. Ross smiled at the look of puzzlement on her face as she felt the cab slowing down.

With a sudden giggle she grabbed his fingers, forcing them away from her eyes.

He clamped them back, pulling her tight against his chest.

'Oh, no, you don't. Two minutes and then you can look.'

Ross held his breath as her heat mingled with his. What would she do if he turned that delectable face towards his and covered her lips with his own?

'OK, mate, where do you want me to stop?'

Ross cursed inwardly as the taxi driver's voice crashed into his thoughts.

'Just at the end of this road. There should be room for you to turn round and go back the way you came.'

Alison gave a little wriggle. 'Can I look now?'

Ross dropped his hands as the taxi slowed to a halt at the end of a narrow road bordering an isolated stretch of beach. 'I don't see why not.'

The restaurant manager had done him proud. In the shelter of a curve of rock, a huge white parasol blocked the last remaining rays of the evening sun, showcasing the table for two set out beneath it. Ross couldn't stop smiling. The light glinting on the silverware and crystal . . . the tablecloth fluttering in the gentle twilight breeze . . . the rhythmic rush of the waves in the background. Everything was so . . . right.

Alison blinked, then gasped. 'Is this for us?'

'I don't see anyone else, do you?' he murmured as the driver moved round the car to open Alison's door.

She climbed out and waited for Ross to join her. 'It's . . . like something out of a Hollywood movie.'

The delight on her face warmed Ross down to his toes.

'Don't tell me you've never had a picnic on the beach before?' he asked her grinning.

A waiter appeared and escorted them across the damp sand.

'A picnic!' Alison echoed as they approached the table. 'As in gritty sandwiches and flasks of tea?'

'As in seafood platters,' Ross supplied, as they settled in their chairs. 'Or if you'd prefer — prawns and smoked salmon. Just ask for whatever you fancy.

I'm sure the restaurant will come up with it.'

The waiter placed a menu in front of each of them, then poured champagne into fluted crystal glasses.

Alison's eyes widened. 'Ross, you know you didn't need to go to all this trouble for me?'

He shook his head. 'You gave Jon a meal to remember and I wanted to do the same for you.'

'So this wasn't just a ploy to stir up my spontaneity?'

Guilt niggled. Yesterday wasn't the first time he'd poured scorn on her ideas and tried to force her to go against her instincts. Yet he'd hated it when the boys' grandmother had used the same approach with him.

'Alison, what I said the other day about you being in a rut . . . I had no right to talk to you like that, and I'm sorry.'

'Don't be.' She pushed her hair back from her face and looked at him. 'Finding my spontaneity spark is really brightening up my life. I'm not quite ready to burn my planners, but I'm getting there. Now for another risk. Shall I have a white or a wholemeal roll with my starter?'

There was a sparkle in her eyes that set the tone for the rest of the meal. The banter flowed between them as they tackled one delicious dish after another, as relaxed as two old friends.

'So, why didn't you tell me you're a doctor?' Alison asked as they sipped their end of meal coffee. 'And don't say the opportunity didn't arise,' she warned, her eyes creasing in a teasing grin. 'That day I knocked Mark over, I was really worried that I'd hurt him. Knowing you're a doctor would have put my mind at rest straight away.'

'Yeah, I'm sorry about that.' He avoided her gaze and concentrated on tracing imaginary circles on the table-cloth. 'I suppose I didn't want you asking the question on everyone else's lips.'

'Which is?'

With a sigh, he raised his eyes to hers. 'How come someone who managed to get through medical school can't cope with looking after a bunch of little kids?'

She regarded him from under her lashes, her mouth twitching with a smile. 'Things will improve, you know. The boys won't always be such hard work.'

'You reckon?'

'Of course. There are signs of improvement already. Their behaviour is a lot more settled than it was a few days ago.'

'I think we both know that any change is down to your organisational skills.'

She slid him a sideways glance. 'I'd like to think some of them are rubbing off on you.'

'I'm trying, Ally,' he said after a long silence. 'But it's time to face facts. I'm no Mrs Doubtfire and never will be. When we leave you, I'll be floundering again.'

'But you'll only be next door.' Some of the teasing light faded from her eyes. 'Didn't you say you're here for the next three months?'

He looked away. 'I might have to rethink that. Maybe once I'm walking again, I should try a bit harder to settle the boys with a nanny and go back to what I'm good at.'

He searched her gaze for some tiny flicker of reaction that would tell him she didn't want him to leave.

Nothing.

For a moment he almost yielded to the urge to blurt out his feelings, tell her he couldn't imagine a future without her, ask if she felt anything for him at all. But that would mean risking the tentative friendship they'd built, and that was one risk too far.

'What about your plans to travel the world and give the boys a childhood to remember?'

'They're not ready for that kind of lifestyle,' he said on a sigh, 'and I'm not sure that I can prepare them.'

She bit her lip. 'You can't give up on your dreams now, Ross. Not when you've come so far.'

Her words caught him unawares. He'd expected a murmur of agreement, a tight little I-told-you-so smile. Certainly nothing like this huge measure of support.

'Not far enough. It doesn't take a genius to see that your routine-based lifestyle has done more to calm them down than any of my wacky ideas.'

She looked at him with a curious expression. 'A few days ago you had faith in those ideas. What went wrong?'

'I realised a few things, I suppose.'

'What sort of things?'

He fiddled with the salt pot. 'When I took over the boys' care, they had so much pent-up anger you could almost scrape it off the walls. So I encouraged anything that helped them let off steam — kicking footballs, climbing trees, charging up and down the garden . . . but that day they found Ben's teddy bear, I saw that all I'd done was give them permission to behave badly, without any thought for anyone else.'

'Oh.'

She seemed disappointed, although he couldn't think of any reason why she should. He was admitting she was right.

'So you thought you'd give my ideas a go?'

Her voice had lost some of its sparkle.

'Yes, and I'm pleased I did. It made me realise that a calm, ordered environment is what they need most right now, not a trip around the world.'

She shifted in her chair. Looked at him. Looked away, her eyes fixed on the crashing waves.

'And you really think handing their care over to a nanny will provide that?'

'A nanny, a good school . . . all I know is I got it wrong and can't put it right on my own.'

'Even if all they need is a clear set of goals?'

He gave a wry smile. 'Somehow I don't think it's that simple.'

'Don't be so quick to put yourself down. There's a lot of sense in what you were trying to do. With a few adjustments, I believe your ideas could work.'

He raised a disbelieving eyebrow. 'Really?'

'Yes, really,' she said, clasping her hands in front of her. 'Would you like me to go on?'

'Please do.'

'Your energy-busting activities involve the boys flailing aimlessly about with no clear goal in mind.'

He leaned back in his chair and folded his arms across his chest. 'Don't sugar it up, tell it to me straight.'

'Oh, I will. What they need is something to show them the benefits of completing a task — working in the garden, helping with the decorating or cleaning the car. You'd need to give lots of encouragement, of course, and make the tasks seem exciting. Then once they've learned to co-operate and see things through, they can move on to the more adventurous stuff . . . fishing, sailing, putting up a tent.'

He didn't reply. He couldn't. Time after time, Ally had come to his rescue without expecting anything back in return. In the short time he'd known her, she'd become a vital part of his life. He loved her.

'It's worth a try, isn't it?' she urged, her sparkling silver eyes doing terrible things to his blood pressure. 'By the time your cousin needs her house back, the boys could be ready for that round-the-world trip after all.'

He leaned across the table and took her hand in his. 'You're amazing, Ally. Do you know that?' he asked in a low, husky voice he didn't recognise. 'I've lost count of the times you've helped me out. I want you to know how much I appreciate it.'

She tipped her head to one side and regarded him with those beautiful eyes. 'Hey, it hasn't been completely one-sided. Helping with the boys has been good for me, too. Given me something new to think about.'

Shaken up her well-ordered world, more like. Brought more pain than she was willing to admit. How like her to sideline her own problems and try to make him feel better about himself.

'You don't have to pretend. I know how difficult it's been for you having the boys around. I'm sorry I put you through that.'

'Don't apologise, Ross. I mean what I say. The experience has helped me feel at ease with children again. Made me realise what I've been missing for the last three years. In fact . . . I'm enjoying it.'

'Enough to do it permanently?'

'What do you mean?'

'Marry me, Ally.'

As soon as the words were out, he wished them unsaid. Instead of taking things slowly and giving her time, he'd done the one thing guaranteed to drive her away. What an idiot!

Stunned disbelief flickered across her features. 'Why?'

Because of words she wouldn't want to hear. She was afraid of involvement, for heaven's sake. He shouldn't even think of using the 'L' word.

'To give the boys a secure family life,' he said, rushing into speech. 'No pressure or expectations, I promise. Just me and you building the boys a happy family life.'

He searched her face for some sign that he hadn't just made a complete fool of himself, but saw only bewildered dismay in her eyes.

The silence lengthened. She bit her lip then slowly shook her head and looked away.

Ross sucked in a long, uneven breath. He didn't have to wait for her to say it to know she'd just turned him down.

A trill from his mobile phone saved her the bother.

He dropped her hands, turned away and answered it. No need for her to witness his disappointment.

A Misunderstanding

Alison blinked before her eyes could fill with hot, angry tears. Pride wouldn't allow her to reveal how much Ross's careless words had stung her. She loved him, longed to share his life, but not like this. The only proposal she wanted from Ross was one that came with love, not an invitation to a marriage of convenience.

His worried tone cut through her thoughts: 'Don't worry, Maria. I'll be right there. I'm only five minutes away.'

Alison's skin went cold. 'Is it one of the boys — '

'It's OK. No-one's hurt. Jon's had a bit of a scare and locked himself in one of the bedrooms. Maria's spent the last hour trying to talk him out.'

Neither of them said much on the journey home.

When they reached Alison's house,

Ned was waiting at the gate.

'Ross, I'm so sorry, mate.' Ned pulled open the car door and took Ross's crutches while he hoisted himself out. 'We were having a quick game before they went to bed, when Jon suddenly screamed and raced upstairs. Maria's up there now with the other three, trying to persuade him to come out.'

Ross retrieved his crutches and swung forward.

'Which bedroom is he in?'

'He ran into the first one he came to — the big one at the front.'

The big room at the front was Alison's room.

Ross hopped to the bottom of the stairs, handed Alison one of his crutches, then grabbed the stair rail while he used the other crutch to aid his climb. Alison followed him, while Ned stood awkwardly in the hall.

Maria greeted them on the landing, with a small embarrassed smile.

'I'm sorry, Ross. The evening was going so well until Ned decided to teach them how to play, 'What's the time, Mr Wolf?', and everything went downhill from there.'

'Tell Ned not to worry.' Ross grabbed the newel post and hauled himself on to the landing. 'Jon's got a bit of a phobia about wolves. But Ned wasn't to know that.'

Maria paused while Ross took his other crutch from Alison and settled it under his arm. 'Perhaps Ned and I should go now. Too many cooks and all that.'

'Yeah. Thanks for coming, Maria. I'll give you a call and we'll all meet up one night. We never did get chance to catch up.'

As Maria left, Ross turned to the boys. 'Let's have you lot downstairs too. I need to talk to Jon without any interruptions.'

'We're worried about him,' Mattie protested. 'When Ned growled, Jon got really, really scared.'

A whimper sounded from behind the bedroom door.

Ross moved forward. 'It's all right, Jon. I'm here now. Open the door.'

'The big bad wolf's gone now,' Mattie called. Then added with a snigger, 'Uncle Ross chopped his head off.'

Jon's whimpers turned into a dramatic wail.

Ross whirled on the boys. 'Sit!' Instantly they obeyed. 'One more word out of any of you and you all go straight to bed. Is that understood?'

'Yes, Uncle Ross,' they whispered in unison.

Ross rapped sharply on the door.

'Right, Jon, time to come out. You've been in there long enough.'

Silence.

'Come on, Jon. Open the door.' There was pleading in Ross's voice.

Ross's gaze flickered to Alison and she looked away.

She wouldn't interfere. It was high time Ross began practising the things she'd taught him, and after their disastrous dinner, she doubted he'd stick around for any more tips. She bit her lip, stemming the fresh surge of pain that clamped around her heart.

'I mean it, Jon. I've had enough of this nonsense. Open this door or — '

The boys exchanged worried looks.

Alison held her breath.

'Or what?' asked a defiant little voice from the other side of the door.

'Or you'll miss your ice-cream,' Ross said after a short pause.

Alison sucked in a breath. Uh-oh, the bribery route. Not good.

'Don't want ice-cream.'

Ross's brows came together in a frown.

Please don't ask Jon what he *does* want, Alison silently urged.

'That's fine,' Ross kept his voice low. 'We're going downstairs now. You can come with us, or stay in there. If you come out now there'll be time for ice-cream before bed. If you stay where you are, there won't be.'

He had hardly finished repositioning his crutches before the door opened and Jon rushed on to the landing.

'That's not fair. Where's my ice-cream?'

Alison gave a small, satisfied sigh and headed for the stairs.

'I'll go and dish it up. I suppose the rest of you would like some, too?'

'Yesss!'

'With chocolate sprinkles?'

The chorus was deafening.

★   ★   ★

Alison, perched on a stool, was rummaging through the cupboard for the chocolate sprinkles when Ross and the boys appeared in the kitchen doorway. She avoided Ross's gaze, the awkwardness between them now stronger than ever.

A pounding of feet and a scraping of chairs told her that at least part of the family was sitting around the kitchen table. A glance out of the corner of her eye showed Ross still standing in the doorway with Jon.

She couldn't bring herself to look at him. How was she supposed to act around a man whose marriage proposal she'd all but turned down? She continued to move tins and jars around the cupboard, even though the sprinkles were right there in front of her.

'Come on, Jon, sit down with your brothers,' Ross prompted.

She heard the thump of Ross's crutches as he joined the boys.

'Where's Ned?' A hint of fear laced Jon's words.

'I told you, he went home.'

Ross must have given the boys another warning glance, as none of them spoke.

'So, what did you do in Ally's bedroom then, Jon?'

'I drew pictures.'

Ross released an uneasy laugh. 'Not on Ally's walls, I hope?'

The little boy giggled. 'No. In my drawing book.'

Ross's tone was playful. 'Go and fetch it then and show us your pictures.'

'He's got it with him, Uncle Ross,' Mark whispered. 'Look. He's hiding it under his pyjama top.'

'Come on, Jon, let's see this amazing artwork.'

The sound of turning pages filled Ally's ears as she continued rummaging in the cupboard.

'Where did you get this book, Jon?' Ross's tone had lost its teasing edge.

'I found it.'

'Where?'

'Under Ally's bed.'

No. Please, no! The tub of sprinkles slipped from Ally's grasp and landed with a dull thud on the floor. Nobody moved or spoke. Fear's stranglehold on her throat closed tighter.

Slowly she turned round. Ross met her gaze.

'Alison?'

He held Claire Samuels' business card in one hand, her open notebook in the other. 'Where did you get these?'

She looked away, unable to bear the hurt and disappointment in his eyes.

'It — it's not what it seems.'

'Really?' His voice was as dead and bleak as his eyes.

'I didn't — I haven't . . .'

But even as she opened her mouth she knew there was nothing she could say to explain this away. She could only stand silently and watch as he turned the pages.

'*'This man really doesn't have a clue*,' he read aloud, '*'has no routines, no boundaries, no proper bed times . . .*'' His facial expression hardened. 'I'd say this is exactly what it seems.'

He snapped the book closed.

'Joining our family was never on the cards, was it, Alison? You weren't interested in us. You were just gathering information for *her*.' He shook his head and gave a humourless laugh. 'So how much is she paying you?'

Regret and anguish clogged her throat. 'She isn't . . . I'm not — '

He tossed the book on to the kitchen table and snatched up his crutches.

'Come on, kids, it's time to move

back next door. We'll collect our stuff later.'

'But what about our ice-cream?' Jon's bewildered voice asked.

'We've got some in our own freezer.'

The boys looked from Alison to Ross. Then, looking lost and sad, they did as they'd been told. Except for Mattie, who ran in the opposite direction.

'I need to get something,' he called over his shoulder. 'I'll catch you up.'

'You've got ten seconds,' Ross bellowed as he ushered the boys outside.

Alison climbed off the stool. Her fingers trembled and her legs shook beneath her. Grabbing a dustpan and brush from the cupboard under the sink, she bent to sweep up the scattered sprinkles.

She should go after him. And tell him what? That he'd got it wrong? That she loved him and the boys and would never do anything to hurt them?

'Ally — ' said Mattie's voice at her elbow. He thrust a plastic supermarket bag towards her. 'It's a present from all of us. Uncle Ross said I had to keep it hidden in my room and give it to you when it was time to go back next door.'

She looked past him into the darkness beyond, unable to bring herself to explain that Ross had expected to leave under more pleasant circumstances.

'Thank you, Mattie. That's very kind.'

'Aren't you going to open it?'

Alison reached inside the plastic bag and withdrew a wooden frame.

'A family photo?'

Mattie shook his head. 'Turn it over.'

All the air in her lungs seemed to rush out. She grabbed for the counter so she wouldn't collapse. Nothing could have prepared her for this. In the middle of a rich red and gold crackle-varnish frame, sat Ben's drawing of Pusskins. The paper's rips and tears had somehow been patched together, its warm coffee tinted background looking for all the world as if it was meant to be that way. Ross had mended Ben's picture along with her shattered heart.

Mattie beamed fit to burst. 'Isn't Uncle Ross clever? I wanted to help, but he wouldn't let me. He said it had to be perfect. Do you like it?'

Not trusting her voice, Ally could only nod.

'I'd better go now. We'll still see you, won't we? Even though we're not sleeping here any more?'

She cleared her throat and somehow managed a smile. 'I hope so, Matt.'

He bounded across the kitchen and out of the door, leaving Alison alone with her picture.

She ran her fingers over Ross's handiwork. A tiny thread of hope shimmered inside her. Would he have gone to all this trouble for a woman he had no feelings for? A woman he saw as mere convenience? She didn't know. But finding out would mean sacrificing every last shred of dignity.

Her heart thudding against her ribs, she grabbed Claire Samuels' notebook and dashed out of the back door. But she'd barely reached the flower border separating the two cottages when Ross's furious voice filled her ears.

'I'm tired of your questions. Just go — and give me some peace!'

Her heart turned over. Those poor kids. He should be taking his anger out on her, not them.

She quickened her pace, reaching the open door just as his voice rang out again.

'So, what are you waiting for?'

She pushed the door wide. 'Ross, that's not fair. You can't — '

The words froze on her lips as Claire Samuels whirled to face her.

'Oh, I'm sorry. I thought . . . the boys . . . '

Heat rushed under her skin as the words tailed off. Could things get any worse?

Claire closed her eyes and pressed her fingers against them, the sudden action making her seem far older and less imposing than the determined businesswoman of a few days earlier.

'The boys are in the living-room eating ice-cream. While their uncle sits here in a sulk.'

Ross rested his elbows on the table and rubbed the back of his neck. 'I'm not sulking, Claire. I've had a harrowing evening, that's all.'

Claire ran her fingers through her hair. 'You and me both.'

Ross sighed. 'Then why are you here?'

'Because my grandchildren need me.'

Ross looked from Claire to Alison with knowing eyes.

'Oh, I get the picture. You two have been exchanging notes and now you're ganging up on me.'

Claire waved a dismissive hand. 'What are you talking about? I'm here because Matt called me.' She angled Alison a concerned glance. 'It was a very panicky call, telling me that his uncle had gone out for the evening, leaving the boys alone and Jon locked in his bedroom.'

Alison touched Claire's arm.

'Do you really think Ross would go out and leave Jon locked in his room?'

Claire frowned, her eyes still thoughtful. 'What was I supposed to think, with poor Mattie nearly incoherent with worry and Jon screaming in the background?'

Ross straightened and wrapped his arms across his chest. 'That you'd misunderstood Mattie's garbled message? That before you came high-tailing it up here, you should phone back and ask to speak to an adult?'

'Would it have made any difference if I had?'

He released a long-suffering sigh.

'Of course it would. I left those boys in the care of a responsible babysitter — an experienced paediatric nurse, no less.'

'So why was Jon screaming?'

'Because he got over-excited during a harmless game. OK, there was a bit of a panic when he locked himself in a bedroom. But he was never in any danger and I came home as soon as I heard about it.'

Claire's lips tightened. 'You could have told me that when I first arrived, instead of being so — '

Alison held up her palm. 'Stop it, both of you!'

There was a stunned silence.

'Claire, I can vouch for Ross's story so drop the accusations.'

Claire's eyebrows lifted but she didn't argue.

'Ross . . . ' Alison crossed the kitchen to place Claire's notebook on the table in front of him. 'I came to talk to you about what's written in here, and I'd like Claire to hear what I have to say, too.'

Ross gripped the edge of the table and hauled himself up. 'You can both take the book next door and compare notes there. I'm going to check on the boys.'

Alison stiffened. He had to listen to her. What she had to say couldn't wait any longer.

'Not until you've heard me out. We can't leave things like this.'

Something flickered in his eyes. Something that told her he wanted stay. To believe in her. That maybe they could work this out.

She held her breath.

'I'm not going anywhere Ross, so you'd better sit down and listen to what I have to say.'

Silent moments slipped by as his deep brown eyes challenged hers.

'I mean it, Ross. I'll stand here all night if I have to.'

Closing his eyes he rubbed at his forehead. Reluctantly he sat back down. Alison took a deep breath to compose herself, moistened her lips and began.

'Claire turned up at my house a few days ago and asked me to keep an eye on you and the boys. The two of us had never met before and knew nothing about each other. But I could see that her concern was genuine . . . ' Her voice tailed off as Ross's eyes darkened.

Claire pulled out a chair and sat

down. 'Go on. We're listening.'

'And if she was right, then I hated the thought of the future awaiting the boys.'

Ross cocked a scornful eyebrow. 'So you decided I was a bad parent — simply on Claire's say-so?'

'Not entirely, no.' She raised her chin. 'I'd already met you by then. And your attitude regarding the boys' bad behaviour didn't do a lot to convince me you were a clued-up and conscientious parent. I was worried that — '

His voice hardened. 'I didn't know how to care for them?'

'Yes.' She picked up the book and held it tightly. 'But then I gradually came to realise that I was wrong.'

His mouth compressed. 'So you contacted Claire to say you could no longer spy for her?' Irony laced his tone.

'No.' Her voice was a husky whisper.

'Then I rest my case.'

Alison swallowed hard before answering. 'Spying was never part of the plan, Ross. I told Claire I'd keep a detached eye on things, and that's all I intended to do.'

'Yet you bought a special book to note your findings.'

'The book was Claire's, not mine, and I accepted it on impulse, never seriously intending to use it.'

Ross gave a bitter laugh.

'But it wasn't long before you did.' He took the book from her, opened it and jabbed at it with his finger. 'The first entry is dated the day we met.'

Alison closed her eyes in pain, remembering how angry she'd been when she'd written those words.

'All right, I admit it. I was so incensed by your laid-back approach to parenting that I grabbed a pen and let the words spill out. But after I'd finished writing, I realised I'd been doing it for me, not Claire, and I had no intention of ever letting her see it.'

He thumbed through the pages. 'Why didn't you call a halt there and toss the book in the bin? Why collect page after page of observations?'

'Confiding in the journal felt helpful and healing,' she managed to say unevenly. 'I found myself going back to it again and again — sometimes two or three times a day. It felt good to get things out of my head and on to paper. Suddenly I could face my fears and express difficult feelings. Open myself up and pour myself on to the page. This wasn't about gathering information to pass on to Claire — it was about organising the thoughts swirling round in my head.'

'Ever considered a career in politics? With your gift for spin, you'd be a natural.'

His mocking smile threw salt on to her wound.

'You don't believe me? Then let me prove it.' She stepped forward and snatched the book from his grasp. 'Here's an entry from day three: '*If I was ever in any doubt that Ross loves his nephews and will always put them first, then today's experience chased those doubts away. Ross fell off a ladder this morning rescuing my cat, and despite the agony of a broken ankle, he refused to go to the hospital unless the boys could go with him.''*

Claire tsked. 'That's just plain foolhardy. What good would he be to them with an untreated fracture?'

Alison stared blankly at her for a moment. 'Maybe he wanted to prove to them that he wasn't about to disappear like their parents. That they could count on him always to be around.'

Claire hesitated, looking a little shame-faced.

'Yes, I can understand that.'

''*Once he'd been treated*',' she continued, her resolve growing stronger with each word, ''*he was determined the boys shouldn't have strangers looking after them, even though he was still in considerable pain. Before I knew what I was doing, I'd invited him and the boys to come and stay with me.''*

Claire frowned. 'There was no need for that. I would have gladly stepped in and — '

'And what, Claire?' Alison looked her straight in the eye. 'Taken the boys back with you, planning to make the arrangement permanent?'

Claire had the grace to blush.

''Having the boys around is difficult for me',' Alison read out, after a slight hesitation, ''after losing Ben. I've never got over it. But by Sunday, with Ross's help, I was beginning to let go.'' Tears sprang to her eyes. She stubbornly blinked them away. ''This man is amazing. When the boys lost their parents he helped them come to terms with their feelings by making pictures and letters for their mum and dad and sending them up into the heavens attached to special memory balloons. Today he and Jon guided me through the process, and for the first time in months I finally feel that I can move forward. Of course, I'll never forget my beautiful Ben.''

Her voice caught. When she looked up, Ross's eyes were filled with tenderness. She met his gaze with hope.

'Can you honestly see this stuff being any good to Claire? Or this: '*And Ross has a gift for making people believe they can deal with anything, however daunting. He might not get the kids to bed on time, cook meals from scratch or attempt any kind of routine, but it doesn't matter. He's offering them something more important — love, of course, and the confidence to face their feelings, to try new experiences and meet life head on.*''

Ross shifted in his chair. 'Ally — '

'I'm not finished.' She held up a hand to silence him. 'If you really want to see how writing helped me gain some perspective, how about this for a change in focus? '*Having Ross and the boys in my life has made me see that I'm the one who has the childcare thing all wrong, not Ross. I've been scared and over-cautious, but with his help I've learned to lighten up. Enjoy life again . . . Even love again. Not just the boys, but their uncle, too. I've . . . fallen in love with Ross, and — *'' Her hands trembled so much she had to set the book down.

'Oh . . . ' Claire broke through the long silence. 'I think I might have done Ross an injustice.'

'Only 'might'?' The twinkle was back in his eyes.

Claire smoothed her hair back from her face. 'All right — I can see I've been a bit quick to believe the worst. And from now on, I'll do my best to ask your side of the story before I make any judgements.'

Kindness softened his eyes and relaxed his jaw.

'Thank you, Claire. That means a lot to me.' He looked at her for a long moment then held out his hand. 'Truce?'

She placed her hand in his.

'Truce,' she repeated, staring at him as if she'd never seen him before.

Then, abruptly, she dropped his hand and stood up. 'You two have a lot to talk about.' She pulled out the chair next to Ross. 'So, why don't you sit here, Alison, while I put the boys to bed?'

She accompanied her matter-of-fact order with a conspiratorial wink.

She refused to budge until Alison complied, then hurried from the kitchen, leaving her sitting beside Ross, not knowing quite what to do or say next.

Was this the point where he told her that her love was one-sided? That he'd never intended her to take things so seriously? The blood pounded in her head so loudly she could hardly think. No, he couldn't do that . . . could he? Not after everything she'd put herself through.

'Tell me, Ally,' he murmured, his crossed forearms on the table as he inclined towards her, 'what were you planning to write as your next entry?'

She licked her dry lips. 'That today I turned down a marriage proposal. Not because I didn't want to accept, but because I could never marry a man who doesn't love me. No matter how much I love him.'

He raised his eyebrows.

'If you truly believe that, why did you

come after me?'

'Because of Ben's picture.' She held a finger against her lips to stop them trembling. 'Mattie gave it to me before he left, and it set me thinking; only a man who felt a deep affection for me could come up with such a perfect present. You don't love me yet, I know, but there's maybe something between us that we can build on. Something that, in time, might turn to love.'

She couldn't shake the anxious dread that seized her stomach.

He looked at her for a moment that seemed to stretch out for ever.

'You're wrong.'

Her body and mind numbed. She'd lost him.

'You don't think you can love me? Ever?'

He reached out and brushed a strand of hair away from her eyes.

'I love you already.'

'You do?' Her heart lifted with a jolt. Warmth slowly trickled back into her veins.

'Is it so difficult to believe?'

He loved her. Her mind was spinning. 'Then why . . . ?'

Ross grasped her hands. 'Did I make such a blundering proposal?' His thumbs brushed her knuckles in a gentle caress. 'A culmination of things, I suppose. The more I got to know about you and your background, the more scared I became of frightening you off. Then tonight at dinner, you looked so lovely and seemed so happy, that the proposal popped out of my mouth before I could stop it.'

'You regretted it.'

He remained silent for a moment.

'Only because I thought you weren't ready for a romantic involvement. I felt so ashamed at pressurising you that I let you think I wanted the marriage for the boys' sakes, when really I wanted it for me.'

She shook her head, blinking away the tears. 'And then I added insult to injury by letting you find that stupid book.'

'I'm glad you did. Without it, I'd

never have realised how you felt.' The warm smile he cast her was both tender and rueful. 'But you're wrong about the childcare thing. It's me that made the mistakes, not you. The boys needed a calmer, more ordered life, and you helped me see that.'

She looked at him from under her lashes. 'Maybe we were both wrong, and together we could get it right.'

He leaned closer and trailed a finger down her cheek.

'Marry me and we'll see.'

Joy bubbled within her.

'Only if we travel the world like you planned.'

'You really want to do that?'

With Ross by her side she was strong enough to tackle anything. She shot him a teasing smile. 'Why wouldn't I?'

'I thought you were against the idea of the boys living on a boat. That sailing dinghies, dodging rocks, and bashing into high seas was far too dangerous.'

The old Alison maybe, but not this one.

'Did I say that?'

'You didn't have to. Cancelling my appointment to view those boats said it all.'

'Boats?' she asked, momentarily at a loss.

'You've developed a conveniently short memory. Do the names Gemma and Susanna ring any bells?'

Her mouth dropped open. 'They're boats?'

'What else would they be?' He regarded her quizzically. 'No . . . you surely didn't think . . . ?'

She eyed him sideways. 'That you'd joined a dating agency? You had a flyer for one on top of the freezer.'

His deep laugh rang out across the kitchen 'I kept a whole bunch of flyers. The kids drew pictures on the backs and wouldn't let me get rid of them.'

The last whisper of doubt faded and she started to laugh too. Without warning he pulled her towards him and silenced her with a long lingering kiss.

When finally he released her, she

drew back and gazed long and deeply into the eyes of the man she loved with all her heart and who she would love for ever.

'Oh, Ross, I have so much to learn about you.'

He slipped his hand behind her neck and drew her close again.

'And I about you,' he murmured against her lips. 'How about we spend the next fifty years teaching each other?'

Alison's sigh was of pure happiness.

'It's a deal.'

The End

We do hope that you have enjoyed reading this large print book.

Did you know that all of our titles are available for purchase?

We publish a wide range of high quality large print books including:
Romances, Mysteries, Classics
General Fiction
Non Fiction and Westerns

Special interest titles available in large print are:
The Little Oxford Dictionary
Music Book, Song Book
Hymn Book, Service Book

Also available from us courtesy of Oxford University Press:
Young Readers' Dictionary
(large print edition)
Young Readers' Thesaurus
(large print edition)

For further information or a free brochure, please contact us at:
Ulverscroft Large Print Books Ltd.,
The Green, Bradgate Road, Anstey,
Leicester, LE7 7FU, England.
Tel: (00 44) **0116 236 4325**
Fax: (00 44) **0116 234 0205**

RETURN TO
HEATHERCOTE MILL

Jean M. Long

Annis had vowed never to set foot in Heathercote Mill again. It held too many memories of her ex-fiancé, Andrew Freeman, who had died so tragically. But now her friend Sally was in trouble, and desperate for Annis' help with her wedding business. Reluctantly, Annis returned to Heathercote Mill and discovered many changes had occurred during her absence. She found herself confronted with an entirely new set of problems — not the least of them being Andrew's cousin, Ross Hadley . . .

THE COMFORT OF STRANGERS

Roberta Grieve

When Carrie Martin's family falls on hard times, she struggles to support her frail sister and inadequate father. While scavenging along the shoreline of the Thames for firewood, she stumbles over the unconscious body of a young man. As she nurses him back to health she falls in love with the stranger. But there is a mystery surrounding the identity of 'Mr Jones' and, as Carrie tries to find out who he really is, she finds herself in danger.